Karin Wallis was a challenge—ah, but she was trouble, too, Xante reminded himself

He stared at the beauty sitting opposite him. Her composure was somewhat restored now, that aloofness back, and Xante wanted more, just a little touch more.

After all—trouble he could handle.

"There is a dinner being held tonight." He watched a frown deepen between her brows, a rare pleasure these days compared to the masklike dates who were usually on his arms. "Given I have just told the security guard that you are my mistress, surely you do not want to disrespect me further...."

"You want me to go to dinner with you?"

"No!" Xante corrected. "I am saying there is no choice other than that you join me. It is a black-tie do and naturally I need an escort. I already had an escort in mind—a couple, in fact—but due to the circumstances I want the woman who will join me tonight, now, to be you."

Carol Marinelli

BLACKMAILED INTO THE GREEK TYCOON'S BED

International Billionaires

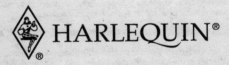

HARLEQUIN®

TORONTO • NEW YORK • LONDON
AMSTERDAM • PARIS • SYDNEY • HAMBURG
STOCKHOLM • ATHENS • TOKYO • MILAN • MADRID
PRAGUE • WARSAW • BUDAPEST • AUCKLAND

Special thanks and acknowledgment
are given to Carol Marinelli for her contribution
to the International Billionaires miniseries.

Recycling programs
for this product may
not exist in your area.

ISBN-13: 978-0-373-23610-7

BLACKMAILED INTO THE GREEK TYCOON'S BED

First North American Publication 2009.

www.eHarlequin.com

Printed in U.S.A.

All about the author...
Carol Marinelli

CAROL MARINELLI finds writing a bio rather like writing her New Year's resolutions. Oh, she'd love to say that since she wrote the last one, she now goes to the gym regularly and doesn't stop for coffee, cake and a gossip afterward; that she's incredibly organized and writes for a few productive hours a day after tidying her immaculate house and taking a brisk walk with the dog.

The reality is Carol spends an inordinate amount of time daydreaming about dark, brooding men and exotic places (research), which doesn't leave too much time for the gym, housework or anything that comes in between. And her most productive writing hours happen to be in the middle of the night, which leaves her in a constant state of bewildered exhaustion.

Originally from England, Carol now lives in Melbourne, Australia. She adores going back to the U.K. for a visit—actually, she adores going anywhere for a visit—and constantly (expensively) strives to overcome her fear of flying. She has three gorgeous children who are growing up so fast (too fast— they've just worked out that she lies about her age!) and keep her busy with a never-ending round of homework, sports and friends coming over.

A nurse and a writer, Carol writes for the Harlequin Presents® and Medical Romance lines, and is passionate about both. She loves the fast paced, busy setting of a modern hospital, but every now and then admits it's bliss to escape to the glamorous, alluring world of her heroes and heroines in Harlequin Presents novels.

For Dad
With love always
Carol xxxxx

CHAPTER ONE

IT WAS her assumption, rather than her arrogance, that first caught Xante's attention.

Wintry London skies were dark, and a rapid-fire of rain had scattered most of the people off the pavements. Even though it was midday, the cars that pulled into the plush forecourt of his hotel had their headlamps on and their wipers swishing furiously. A few braved the weather; coats overhead, they ran back from lunch to their work or their next meeting, while the organised or more seasoned Londoners opened umbrellas and carried on chatting into their phones. Only a select few took refuge in the forecourt of Xante Rossi's Twickenham hotel.

Xante owned several hotels—they were part of his impressive portfolio—but rarely was the man himself to be found standing in their foyers, checking that everything was in order. He had staff to take care of those details. But today was different. Xante had a particular soft spot for his Twickenham establishment—it allowed him to indulge his passion for rugby. Today the England rugby team was arriving for an official function which was being held to raise serious money for charity. *Serious* money. The crème de la crème of high society would be attending the charity auction tonight that would be held at the end of dinner and would prove an opportunity for the rich to publicly display their wealth under the guise of it being for a good cause.

Xante liked all sports, but—unusually, perhaps, for a Greek—rugby was his passion. He loved the noble game; the blood, sweat and toil that made the game great. *Philotimia* was a sense of honour so vital to his people that it was written into the Greek legal code, and for Xante the great game of rugby represented *philotimia* perfectly.

Once the players were all here at his hotel they would train and travel as a team, but for now they were trickling in from across the country, and Xante had already greeted several, including the captain. It was natural that he wanted to be here to personally welcome the team—and it was natural, for entirely different reasons, that he noticed the willowy blonde arrive in the foyer. Svelte and tall, she'd have captured and held any man's attention, and she was holding Xante's now.

It was the way she shrugged off her coat—not with arrogance, just with the assumption that someone would catch it—that told him she was well heeled.

He had chosen his staff well. Albert, his chief concierge, moved quickly, realising that the bell boy had failed to notice her rich aura, and he caught the coat in an impressive move. Then, without a backward glance, the woman walked into the foyer.

Only then did she hesitate.

Taking in her surrounds, green eyes darting, she fleetingly looked a fraction lost, and only then did Xante fathom that she wasn't a guest.

The hotel was practically in lockdown. Xante had brought in many extra staff to ensure that his important guests' privacy was respected. Fans would remain outside, and journalists, however heavily disguised, were at this moment being politely turned away. But this woman, seemingly without prearrangement, had waived scrutiny and waltzed in as if she owned the place.

Certain people did not require a passport, Xante knew, and this lady appeared to be one of them.

She was strolling around the foyer, looking at the artwork on display, presumably waiting to meet someone. Xante's head was full of questions, which meant he required answers—and quickly, please! It was the hallmark of his success.

'That lady.' Xante checked with his concierge, the one person in the place who would certainly know. 'Who is she?'

Albert was talking to a couple, telling them about numerous shows that were on at the West End, before swiftly moving to his desk to check ticket availability. A brilliant multi-tasker, Albert still managed to deliver the required information to his boss as the theatre agent placed him on hold.

'Karin Wallis,' Albert said in low tones, and Xante frowned at the familiar name. His life was too busy to read the who's who of London, Paris or Rome, or wherever his schedule dictated that he be, and he relied on people like Albert to do the groundwork for him.

'Is she famous?' The name *was* familiar. Xante's brow furrowed as he tried to place it.

'She's from one of England's most famous families,' Albert murmured. 'They regularly grace the social pages.'

'And?' Xante pushed, because Albert never volunteered gossip—he always wanted to be asked!

'The parents died a couple of years ago. The brother's a bit of a rogue, but charming; the younger sister attends boarding school.'

'What about Karin?' Xante was tired of squeezing out information. 'What do you know about her?'

'Well, the press refer to her as "the Ice Queen".' Albert gave a tight smile. 'They would argue that the name merely refers to the numerous ski trips the lady takes—she's just returned from one in Switzerland—however…' Albert gave a small cough to show he was uncomfortable discussing such things and reluctant to give his boss advice; it was a dance they performed regularly.

'Go on,' Xante invited.

'Frankly, sir, you'd be wasting your time with her. No one gets close to Karin Wallis.' Always discreet, Albert immediately termi-

nated the conversation as the couple reap-
proached the desk. 'It shouldn't be much
longer now, sir...' Even if Xante was his
boss, the guests came first—that was the
reason Xante employed him, after all.

Xante nodded, heading to Reception,
where he checked in with the floor manager,
reminding him that he wished to be informed
whenever one of the team arrived.

The Ice Queen!

How Xante wished he had time to rise to
Albert's unwitting challenge today. Impossibly good-looking and obscenely wealthy,
Xante Rossi had no trouble attracting women.
Raised on a Greek Island by his widowed
mother, Xante had fought hard just to exist,
scavenging for food in the overflowing bins
outside the restaurants where the rich tourists
ate, scouring the fishing nets for their rotten
remains. His father's death had devastated
him, but on that wretched day, all those years
ago, something else had happened that had
frightened the nine-year-old Xante.

He had been at the beach, waiting for news
with uncles, cousins and friends, whilst his
mother had been back at the house, keeping
vigil, praying for a miracle. Then the boat
had returned with its grim load.

An uncle who had been fishing with Xante's father had broken the harsh news to him, letting the small boy cry for a while before telling him that now he must be strong. The priest had gone to break the news to his mother.

He couldn't remember the walk home. Maybe they had gone in a car; Xante truly couldn't recall.

What he did recall though was the shock of walking into the house and seeing his mother dressed head to toe in black.

She'd only been in her twenties, but that day, in Xante's eyes, she'd aged two decades.

All the colour, all the vibrancy, was wiped away for ever. On that fateful day, he'd lost not just his father but his mother's laughter too. How he had wanted it back. Had wanted her to dress again in pretty floral skirts and white, cotton tops; had wanted her hair in curls instead of hidden behind a black scarf; had wanted her to wear make-up again and had wanted to smell her sweet perfume.

But those days, like his father, had gone for ever.

His mother, the house, shrouded in grief.

But at fourteen Xante had found a diversion.

He'd been tall for his age, good-looking even then, and the tourists that had flocked to his home town had provided rich pickings. The older *kamaki* boys had told him that, having mastered the art of kissing, it was time to move on to the mountains. Riding up on his scooter with a pretty girl who'd worn vibrant colours and make-up, and who'd laughed at his jokes and held tight to his waist, Xante had finally found freedom from the stuffy confines of home.

He had been found out, of course. The school had written to his mother about his poor attendance, and she had called for his uncle, who had located him on the mountain in a rather compromising position. Then Xante had been hauled back home and beaten to within an inch of his life, his mother screaming of the shame he had brought to their family name.

It had put an end to his mischief for a while.

Xante had buckled down at school, and his grades had picked up, but always the mountains had called him.

And still, even today, Xante remembered that surge of triumph he had felt in his *kamaki* days when he had eked a delicious response from virgin flesh, or had aided a lonely housewife to escape the drudgery of the marital bed and discover her most intimate secrets again.

Ice Queen! Xante smiled to himself; there was no such thing.

Still, he was far too busy for distraction today. He took a seat in the guest lounge, where his computer demanded his attention. Coffee was automatically served, but Xante couldn't help but observe the woman in question as she walked into the room.

The vigilant head-waiter immediately guided her to a seat, and for the first time Xante realised she was nervous. Xante read women easily; he had grown up mastering the skill. And, though most would have missed it, Karin Wallis was certainly nervous. Her eyes were darting around the room as she entered, but there was such poise to her that most wouldn't have noticed; all they would have seen was an elegant woman walking in gracefully.

Heads turned as she passed.

Elite sportsmen, who could have and did have the most beautiful women by their sides, noticed her just as Xante had. There was nothing sleazy about it. The women all looked too; there was just something about her that merited more than a passing glance.

Breeding.

That was the word.

Her fine, porcelain features, the elegant way that she sat—her legs slightly to the side, and crossed neatly at her slim ankles—were all noted by Xante.

She wasn't a hotel guest, of that he was now sure. There was no laptop at her side, either, and she wasn't checking her watch as if to meet anyone. In fact, she took the proffered menu, and when Xante heard her crisp, well-schooled voice order tea and a sandwich he realised she intended to eat alone.

His phone bleeped. The call was an important one, as it always seemed to be these days, so he took it, speaking in Greek with his broker. He instantly forgot about the blonde, his mind back on business now—until she stood up. It was a move that unwittingly cost Xante an inordinate amount of money, and he ended the call telling his broker that he would deal with the fallout himself, before promptly switching off his phone.

She was wandering around the room,

staring intently at the small memorabilia-display on the far wall. She'd lost weight recently, Xante surmised. She was wearing a smart, charcoal suit, but her skirt hung just a fraction too low on her slender hips and her jacket was too wide for her shoulders. Still, she was generously curved where it mattered. At the top of those slender legs was a pert bottom, and as she undid her jacket she unwittingly revealed a glimpse of cashmere bosom. It had been unwitting, as there was a slight prudishness to her that appealed to Xante—because, from his extensive experience, there was no greater pleasure than feeling the uptight come undone.

Yes, prudish described Karin Wallis perfectly. She wore little make-up to accentuate her fine features; her thick, blonde hair sat on the nape of her neck, coiled into a low bun. Her cashmere jumper was worn high on her neck, her skirt low on her knees, and her shoes were just a little too flat and heavy to really set off such magnificent legs. But still she was stunning. Still Xante had to look away, reaching for a newspaper and pretending to read for a full five minutes before it could be considered decent to stand.

Busy or not, Xante decided as he crossed the room, there was always time for a beautiful woman.

Karin didn't actually know what she was doing here, or even what she was going to do now that she was.

It had been four weeks since she'd realised the rose was missing. She'd confronted her brother Matthew and had found out that he'd sold it. She'd agreed to sell off yet another painting, an ornate dresser and her late mother's favourite earrings to pay for their sister's final year of schooling—not realising that when she had signed the documents he'd deliberately beguiled her and had added the jewelled rose to the document too.

The ruby-encrusted rose that had been awarded to her grandfather the year the England rugby team had won every game they had played was so much more than a trinket. It had been her grandfather's prized possession—Karin's too. So many times she had escaped the chaos at home to go and spend some time with her widowed grandfather at Omberley Manor, the home she and Matthew now lived in. There had been many afternoons spent listening to the wonderful tales of his glory days, and Karin remembered each one with love. By the time Karin was fifteen, her grandfather had long since washed his hands of his wayward son and wife, and had told Karin that the rose would be hers on his death. For Karin the rose was the last link to her grandfather and to the great man he had been. It also represented everything her family could have been. And, if she protected her sister from the truth just a little while longer, it was a symbol of everything Emily might one day become.

Karin had been frantically searching for the rose for weeks. Next week she had a formal function to attend at Twickenham to celebrate her grandfather's achievements, and it was assumed she would bring the jewel with her, but every attempt to trace it had proven futile. All she knew was that the rose had been sold to an anonymous bidder—the buyer, apparently, had insisted on anonymity—and Karin didn't even know if it was a he or she.

Till this morning.

Karin had been taking her morning coffee-break, sitting in the library-staffroom and reading an article in the newspaper about the start of the Six Nations rugby tournament that was due to begin the following February. A small piece about the lavish hotel in Twickenham where the England rugby team would be for a charity event had caught her eye. It would seem that the owner, a Greek shipping tycoon, had an impressive display of sports memorabilia, she'd read—his latest acquisition, the bespoke ruby-rose.

Karin lived a rigid and ordered life. She chose to; it was better that than succumb to the reckless, gluttonous gene that had ultimately killed her parents and was now wreaking havoc on her brother. She rarely acted on impulse.

But an hour ago she had.

Pleading a sudden migraine, she had grabbed her coat and hailed a taxi—and now here she was, in a place where she could barely afford a sandwich. Appearances to the Wallises were everything, so Karin had ordered refreshments and had sat to draw breath and try to form a plan. And then she had seen it, locked behind glass, just a few metres from where she sat.

It had been cleaned.

As she walked over to examine it, for a moment she wondered if it was *her* rose, but of course it was. In fact, glittering, sparkling and lovingly restored to its pristine glory, it was just as she remembered it from her childhood. Long-ago days when she would press her face to the glass and ask to hold the 'fairy wand', as she had called it. Bending her knees slightly and peering closely into the cabinet, she realised she was practically doing that now.

'My rose is very beautiful, yes?' A low, heavily accented voice reminded her of her surroundings, and Karin quickly straightened up.

'Very,' came her rigid response, her teeth grinding together as this man, who introduced himself as Xante Rossi, dared to tell her some more about it, dared to give her its history. Her head turned in confrontation, especially when he dared to refer to the rose as his.

'Actually…' When finally she faced him, Karin only managed a single word. So violent was her reaction to this man, she felt as if she'd been side-swiped. His black eyes slammed into hers and it felt as though she was falling into a dangerous spin. She wanted desperately to slam on the brakes, to swerve, to do something, but instead she stood for a telling moment, just too stunned to react.

Usually she wore her frozen shield well, but, so focussed had she been on the rose, for a moment she had dropped her guard and utterly lost her aloof facade. Her face was flaming, as in one lingering second she took in the raven hair and the straight Roman nose. But it was the black eyes that continued to hold hers for a fraction longer than was decent, his full, sensual mouth curving into a slight smile as he gauged the intensity of her reaction.

This would take no time at all!

'Here.' He unlocked the display cabinet. Xante did not need to show off, to impress, but somehow he *did* want to impress her. He was quietly pleased with his latest acquisition, the ruby rose the perfect accessory for his top-class hotel. He took no real pleasure in the actual possession of it, or the rest of his memorabilia. It was more that he thrived on the drive it had taken to succeed. But the rose really was exceptionally beautiful, and represented the lion-hearted men of England. Opening the cabinet, he pulled out the trinket.

'It deserves closer inspection; you are welcome to hold it,' Xante said, and Karin blinked, watching as long-fingered, olive-skinned hands unlocked the cabinet. A heavy, expensive watch was revealed beneath the pristine white cuffs of his shirt, the sharp cut of his immaculate suit moving to accommodate wide shoulders as he bent to retrieve the jewel. Even the back of his head was sexy. Jet-black hair, without a single hint of grey, was superbly cut into a delicious point at the back of his neck. As he stood to his impressive height her guard shot up. Hypervigilant now, Karin deliberately didn't look at him. He was flirting, and Karin knew it. She didn't usually look at men like that, didn't invite them in, and with good reason. If he hadn't been handing her the rose, she'd have paid her bill and left, would have terminated contact there and then. Except she could feel the familiar, cool weight of the trinket in her hand.

'Excuse me, sir...' The hotel manager brought welcome diversion for Karin, but not Xante. 'Another player has just arrived.'

'Thank you.' Xante had to go. It was right that he go, but he also wanted to return. It would be rude to take the jewel from her now and lock it up; she was staring at it so intently, enjoying its beauty, just as Xante was enjoying hers. She had the most exquisite eyes, the only flash of colour in her pale face,

a rich turquoise-green; a colour that reminded
Xante of the Aegean Sea of home… Dangerous seas, Xante simultaneously reminded
himself and discounted. She *was* a lady;
Xante was sure of it. In an instant he'd made
up his mind. 'Enjoy…' He gave her another
devastating smile. 'I shall be back in just a
moment.'

CHAPTER TWO

HE'D left her with it.

As Xante walked off, Karin stood reeling at the turn of events. She'd walked in here with no notion or plan, and the owner had just handed the rose to her and left her with it.

It was a sign surely that it was hers to do with as she wished.

Karin had never stolen a thing in her life. Not once had such a thing entered her head. But it entered it now. She had come here on impulse, to plead with the buyer just to see it… She truly didn't know. She had no money to buy it back; her brother Matthew had spent it before Karin had even realised the rose was missing.

And now here it was, in her hands, and this man had no idea who she was…

Her heart was pounding, her head whirring with indecision.

It belonged in her family, Karin frantically reasoned. It had been her grandfather's most treasured possession, and this Greek billionaire with his bags of money had just bid for it! Had just assumed his money gave him the right to own it, to display it… Well, it *wasn't* his!

There was a fire-escape door to her right, but her coat was at Reception.

It was a coat, for heaven's sake… Her mind was racing, sweat beading on her forehead and running between her breasts, as slowly she wandered nearer the door, sure everyone knew what she was contemplating. Glancing around the room, she saw the world appeared to be carrying right on as normal—men laughing, couples chatting, the chinking sound of china as afternoon tea was taken. And, with one last, furtive glance to the lobby, impulse took over for the second time that day.

Pushing open the door, Karin stepped out. The air felt cold and delicious on her burning cheeks, and she ran. Guilt and shame chased her as she dodged people, colliding with them at times, dirty water splashing her stockinged legs; her lungs felt as though they were bursting. Then stars that had been exploding in front of her eyes suddenly went black as her forward movement was rapidly halted by a huge wedge of flesh. Arms wrapped around her from behind as she was expertly tackled and brought down to the floor.

The brute of a man who had felled her, yet who had also partly cushioned her landing, spoke. 'Going somewhere in a hurry?'

Karin recognised him as the England rugby captain, and prayed, just prayed, that he wouldn't recognise her at that moment. She lay in stunned silence, her stockings laddered, her knee grazed and her face muddied as, less than gracefully, he hauled her up to embark on her walk of shame. Karin felt sure that her grandfather must be turning in his grave, as the granddaughter he had so proudly adored was frogmarched back to the hotel by one of his beloved England team.

It was the most humiliating walk of her life, but because it was Xante Rossi's hotel at least the incident was dealt with discreetly—even a common thief was treated with dignity at Xante's establishment.

She was spared the shame of being dealt with in the lobby; instead she and the captain were guided to the manager's office. She could hear the distant sound of police sirens as the door closed; the manager stared at her grimly, the captain eyeing her with utter distaste.

'It's not how it looks,' Karin croaked, still clutching the rose, holding it in her hands, the evidence irrefutable.

'I'd say it's exactly how it looks,' came the captain's surly response.

'Let's just wait for the police,' the manager said politely.

For Xante, most of the event had gone unnoticed. Chatting to his staff and guests, he had been mildly aware of some activity in the lounge, but Albert's well-oiled crisis machine meant that even he hadn't noticed the drama. He had looked over, frowning, when he realised that she wasn't there. His mind was not on the jewel, but the woman; he was more than ready to commence from where he had left off.

And then Albert discreetly told him what had just occurred.

He was incensed.

Not just about the trinket, not just with her, but with himself.

He read women. Apart from making an obscene amount of money, that was what he did best. He had grown up on it, thrived on it, and after his bitter break-up with Athena he had honed his skill and perfected it, determined he would never be beguiled again. Yet Karin Wallis just had.

He would press charges! Xante's face was as black as thunder as he walked unannounced into the manager's office. He would have her prosecuted to the full extent of the law. *Let's see how ladylike she looks being loaded into the back of a police car,* Xante thought as he slammed into the office.

And then he saw her face.

Drained of colour, streaked with mud, her green eyes pleaded with him. Her legs nervously bobbed up and down as she sat, and he took in her grazed and bloodied knee. It was then that Xante remembered where he knew her name from.

Wallis.

The rose he had purchased had been awarded to the late, great Henry Wallis—and now, here before him, was the greedy seller. Even Xante had been taken aback by the high reserve-price that had been placed on the rose, but his appetite had been whetted, and he had paid the inordinate sum. Now it seemed the little vixen had decided she wanted it back.

She made him sick!

'I saw her leaving with it,' the captain explained. 'I chased her.'

'What were you thinking, Karin?' He saw the flash of question in her eyes as to how he knew her name. Xante's mind was working overtime. Henry Wallis was a legend, a legend who deserved protection. His intention had been to press charges, but with the England rugby team staying at his hotel he could do without this type of publicity. No. He stared into Karin's curious eyes and decided he would deal with her himself.

'I'm sorry.' Her teeth were chattering so violently she could barely get the sentence out. 'Please, I'll do anything…'

Which was something to work with, at least!

'My apologies, officer.' He flashed his charming smile to the police officer present. 'We appear to have wasted your time. There's been a misunderstanding.'

'She was caught stealing…'

'We were arguing!' Xante interrupted. 'This is her grandfather's jewel; Karin does not like the fact that I have it on display, do you, darling?' He watched her nervous swallow and smiled his black smile at her. 'She feels it cheapens his memory.'

'You're Karin Wallis?' The England captain winced in recognition. 'Of course you are. I'm so sorry…'

'You were not to know,' Xante assured him, rapidly clearing things up as Karin sat there reeling. 'Come.' He offered her his hand, his face smiling; only she could see the dangerous glint in his eyes. 'We'll go upstairs and sort this out.'

She didn't have much choice, but for an instant Karin actually considered calling the police back and confessing; anything was preferable to going up to this man's room. She could sense his anger, sense danger, and for Karin it was terrifying. As they stood in the lift, his black eyes bored into her. She stood rigid, refusing to look at him, fingering the scar on her wrist and wondering how she could possibly extricate herself from this mess. Thinking of her sister Emily at boarding school, and the very public humiliation she would have suffered had Xante Rossi pressed charges.

'Sit down,' he ordered when they reached their destination, but not unkindly. He poured her a large glass of water from a jug and watched as she drank. He refilled her glass, before taking himself to his desk and sitting directly opposite her.

'Are you okay?'

Funny, given the circumstances, that he cared enough to ask. But Karin was strangely touched that he had. 'I'd like to apologise.' She tried to look him in the eye, except she couldn't. 'For the misunderstanding.'

'Karin.' Xante halted her there. 'We both know the truth, remember? You came here with every intention of stealing the rose.'

'No.' Karin pleated the hem of her skirt with her fingers, wondering how to possibly explain the moment of madness that had come over her. 'I came here to talk with you. I'm supposed to be attending a function on Saturday at Twickenham to honour my grandfather. It was his rose, and I'm expected to bring it—only it was stolen from my home; I've been trying to track it down...' Karin knew that if she were strapped to a lie detector it would be smoking now. Could almost see the needle waving frantically as she spoke, and, worse, she knew that Xante knew she was lying. 'I never intended to steal it, it was...' His black eyes just stared and she willed him to halt her, but he didn't. 'It was just on impulse. I'm probably not making much sense.'

'Take your time.' Xante gave her a thin smile. 'I'm not in any rush.'

'I'm sorry, okay?'

'For lying or for stealing?'

'I'm telling the truth.'

'Could I just say something here?' Xante stared at the top of her head as she lowered her burning face. 'I believe handling stolen goods is an offence—have you heard of that, Karin?'

'Yes.'

'Which is one of the reasons I am extremely careful in all the acquisitions I make. This is all rather worrying; my buyer is normally meticulous with his background checks.' He stood up and headed over to a filing cabinet, chatting politely, but all the while twisting the knife. 'You reported the theft of the rose to the police, I assume?'

Bastard!

The word boiled inside her. Sitting up in the chair, she lifted her head, her chin set in defiance; she refused to let him see her shame.

He handed her a sheet of paper, but Karin didn't take it. She didn't even look at it; she knew exactly what was written there. 'Is that your signature?'

'I thought I was signing just for the painting,' Karin attempted, but she knew it was hopeless. What would he care that Matthew had duped her? Why sit and shame herself further by admitting that she was trying to run a stately home on an assistant's wage, and that they'd agreed to sell the painting to pay for Emily's school feels because there was no money left?

'So it wasn't, as you earlier said, stolen?' Xante persisted.

'Clearly not.'

'So it *is* mine?'

She ground her teeth together. It wasn't his; technically, legally, it was his, but still she couldn't bring herself to admit it.

'It *is* mine, Karin,' he answered when she didn't. 'You sold it, and just because you've suddenly changed your mind, just because you're a spoilt little rich girl used to taking whatever she wants and getting her own way, it doesn't alter the fact that the rose now belongs to me. Had you chosen to discuss this rationally, then maybe we could have come to some agreement.'

Xante stared at the rose on his desk, and wondered what had possessed her to part with it in the first place. He couldn't believe the beautiful, elegant woman that had walked into his hotel less than an hour ago had so easily fooled him.

'I made a mistake today.' Her voice was as clear as a bell now. Karin was frantically trying to regain control, to salvage what she could from this appalling situation, but she refused to bow to tears. She was sitting straight in the chair, her hands neatly in her lap, staring back at him as if *she* were the one conducting the interview. 'The rose means a lot to the Wallis family; there is a lot of history behind it. I don't expect you understand.'

'Why?' A small coil of black smoke seemed to be rising inside him. Any sympathy that had doused his anger evaporated, as so coolly she stared back at him.

'There's a lot of tradition.'

'Karin.' He halted her there and then. 'Greeks have tradition and history too, but in any culture a thief is a thief.'

'Will you press charges?'

'I am not going to waste the police's time again.'

'What about the rose?' Karin asked, but Xante just smiled.

'Ah, that's right, you have a function next

Saturday.' He appeared to think about it, his shrewd eyes narrowing for a moment, and then he merely shrugged. 'I will make a deal with you. You give me your number, and if it goes back on the market you'll be the first to know.'

It was pointless, because she couldn't afford it anyway, but rather than admit that she duly wrote her number down.

'Well, thank you.' She couldn't believe she was getting away so lightly, but even as she made to stand she soon realised her mistake.

'I haven't finished yet, Karin.'

'I don't see that there's anything else to discuss…'

'Oh, but there is.' There were several women waiting for Xante's summons, all vying for their place on his arm tonight—but Xante suddenly felt it *appropriate* that he arrive tonight with Henry Wallis's grand-daughter on his arm. He told himself it had nothing to do with the instant flare of approval he had seen in the England captain's eyes when he had realised who Karin was.

'There is a formal dinner here tonight in aid of charity.' He watched a frown deepen between her brows—a rare pleasure to observe these days compared to the botoxed dates that usually graced his arms. 'Given I have just implied to everyone that you are my mistress, there is no other way.'

'You want me to go to dinner with you?'

'No,' Xante corrected. 'There was someone I *wanted* to take to dinner tonight, but due to the circumstances, unfortunately, it now has to be you.'

'But why would you take me? I tried to steal…'

'You would have to be extremely stupid to try again. Anyway, you have left me with no choice. There is no question of my going alone and, thanks to your performance downstairs, it is now assumed we are an item.'

'And it's just dinner?' Karin checked.

'In a moment you will no doubt go to tidy yourself…' Xante mocked her with a black laugh. 'And, when you do, please consider my vantage point when you posed that question. I can assure you, dinner will more than suffice!'

'I'll go home and get ready.'

He halted her as she stood. 'Forgive me if I appear mistrusting, but you will get ready here, I think.'

'I didn't exactly come dressed for a five-star ball!'

'There is a beauty salon downstairs; I will have some clothes sent over from a boutique.' He gave a thin smile at her raised eyebrows. Clearly, she thought, this man was used to grooming women. 'I will take you to my suite.' He must have seen her tense, because he answered her unspoken thoughts straight away. 'I will shower and change in here. I will come for you at seven.'

As easy as that, he sorted it. He took her along the corridor, and she entered a vast, luxury suite. One of the perks of living in a five star hotel, Karin realised, was that one was always ready for unexpected guests. Her heels sank into the thick carpet, her eyes taking in the gleaming furnishings. Karin was used to being surrounded by nice things, and shouldn't really have been so overwhelmed, but it only highlighted what her home was lacking. These things were tended to and lovingly polished; the thick, heavy drapes no doubt didn't shoot a layer of dust when drawn, like the ones at home.

'I'll ring the boutique; they will send someone over. If you don't mind organising your appointment at the salon?'

'Will I get a booking?' Karin glanced at her watch. Four p.m. on a Friday afternoon wasn't exactly the ideal time to book in for a complete overhaul.

'You are ringing from my room," Xante said. 'Nothing will be too much trouble.'

And then he left.

Karin half-expected a puff of smoke to linger in his absence. If only she had three wishes!

Well, not spending the night in jail might count as one, Karin conceded as she rang down to the salon and was told that someone would be with her within the hour.

The boutique was just as rapid to coop- erate, despatching a choice selection of clothes, along with an assistant. Karin declined the assistant's help, and tried on the dresses in the privacy of the spacious bathroom, selecting a heavy, blush- coloured velvet that fitted like a glove. When Karin's hair had been blasted into submission, her face, hands and feet all painted and pretty, she accepted that, given how frugally she'd tried to live these past couple of years, she'd just maybe unwit- tingly got her second wish.

The beautician held up her gown. She was

now coiffed and made up; time was moving on. 'Let me help you into your dress.'

'I can manage from here, thank you,' Karin said primly.

'But the zip…'

'I'll be fine.' Karin's crisp voice was non-negotiable. Finally alone, dressed in the hotel's bath-robe, Karin stared at her reflection and hardly recognised herself. She'd always been more into books than make-up, and her dress style was usually conservative at best. With good reason.

But she knew tonight she'd attract stares. She always had, in some respects. That wasn't vanity talking; her face and name were recognisable even when she made no effort. But with her hair so spectacularly pinned, and her make-up skilfully applied, she was honest enough with herself to know that she looked good. Attractive, even. Sexy, perhaps…

It wasn't the stares that worried her, though, it was Xante.

She'd never had such a violent attraction to a man; even David, who she had been with for months, had never affected her in that toe-curling way Xante had. In that instant, when he had first come over before her foolish actions, there had been this shock of attraction, which now as the hour approached she couldn't erase from her mind.

Karin swallowed down a rush of nerves that swarmed like butterflies in her throat as she peeled off her dressing gown.

Trying not to look in the mirror, she pulled on the French-lace panties and lacy, strapless bra she had chosen. They were beautiful, the black lace against the sheer pink, the little beads in the centre. But Karin loathed them. Their beauty and fragility only accentuated the unsightly thick scarring that laced an ugly network on her lower chest, thick bubbles of skin where the hot metal of the car wreckage had seared her flesh. The surgeon had told her, when her wounds had settled, that something possibly could be done to disguise them—only nothing ever had been.

Her parents had been loath to discuss the circumstances of the car accident and push for further treatment, and in turn Karin had been reluctant to show her body and live the nightmare again. It had been far easier just to cover the scars and pretend they didn't exist.

Except they did exist.

And, no matter what the self-help books had said about the topic—that she should love herself and the rest would follow; that a loving man would accept her, faults and all—it actually didn't work like that. Because she'd trusted David, had told him her past when he'd insisted on hearing it, had shown him her scars when he'd assured her it wouldn't change anything. Only it had.

Over and over, despite repeated, desperate attempts, he had rejected her in the most intimate way possible.

Karin and her dashing army captain, society's rising golden-couple, had, as the papers had said, 'amicably' parted. Yet there had been nothing amicable about the fresh batch of scars David had left her with—emotional scars, that were as deep and as raw as the ones on her body.

A thick, mascara-laced tear slid down her cheek, and Karin quickly dabbed at it. No one must ever guess that for now her life was anything but perfect.

For Emily's sake.

So she pulled on the dress and stood, seemingly resplendent, draped in full-length blush-velvet that hugged her curves, the heavy halter-neck jacking up her bosom. Her cleavage was only slightly revealed, but with bare arms too it felt as if acres of flesh were on show; all Karin felt was exposed.

Hearing the knock on the door, Karin took a deep breath and held it as Xante entered the room. She stared into those black eyes and felt a flutter of something unfamiliar deep inside. Her own arousal unnerved her. She'd never found it easy to look a man in the eye, only with Xante she wanted to, and that was what scared her. His dark, brooding good looks did nothing to soothe her; she could almost smell the testosterone in the air that surrounded them. Karin knew that, despite the luxury suite and the designer suit, despite all the trappings, Xante was a bad boy made good. Instantly she was on the defensive. She picked up a small, jewelled bag and dropped her lip gloss in before giving him a brittle smile.

'Right; let's get this over with.'

'Karin…' His low voice, his thick accent, seemed to stroke her inside, turning her into a mess of nerves. But she hid it well, meeting his eyes with icy defiance. 'We can have a long, miserable night exchanging barbs, resenting every minute we are together, or we can try and enjoy this evening.'

She gave a terse nod.

'You look very beautiful.'

'Thank you.' How clipped and formal she sounded, compared to his languorous ease. Utterly comfortable dressed to the nines, he was a man completely at ease with his potent sexuality, and Karin would have killed for just an ounce of his confidence. 'So do you.' Her words were wooden, her smile forced, and, closing her bag, she crossed the room and walked out to the mirrored lift.

Even if it was more for the guests' benefit than hers, she was rather grateful when his hand found hers. Hot and warm, it closed around hers, and she gripped him back.

'You'll be fine.' Just as the lift hit the lobby, he turned and smiled at her, and offered her reassurance—the same smile that had greeted her when they'd first met, a smile that wasn't mocking or superior, just welcoming.

As the lift door opened and they stepped out as a couple, Karin was careful not to make her third wish.

Xante Rossi was no doubt used to dating the world's most beautiful women. If he'd known her past, if he knew her present, he would never truly want her.

It was imperative she keep her distance.

Removing her hand, she turned her attention to the guests and did what she always did when duty called—she sparkled.

CHAPTER THREE

BY THE time seven p.m. came round, Xante was seriously questioning his decision to have Karin escort him tonight.

He had looked her up, of course. Xante had already known about her grandfather's achievements—Henry Wallis's stunning rugby-career was legendary—but he had found himself reading further on and discovering more. Henry had an only child—a son, George—who'd had a charmed life too; attending the best schools, studying and attaining a law degree, then being called to the bar. The Wallis name had continued to shine brightly; George had married the stunning society-beauty Sophia, and together they had produced three ravishing blonde children. They had been the talk of London. Sophia had been a high-profile patron of many charities, quietly supporting her husband's non-existent career—to Xante's trained eyes, anyway. An invitation to a famous Wallis party had been, Xante had read with an ironic smile, an invitation to join the elite of London society.

Yet even fairy tales had their dark side. There had been the odd salacious article that had always been quickly refuted by the Wallis family's spin-doctors. George Wallis had been furthering his studies, or working on an international case, not drowning in alcohol and debt. But the occasional chink had certainly appeared in the solid Wallis armour. Still, all had been forgiven when two years ago their charmed, golden lives had come to an untimely end as the result of a boating accident. Their only son Matthew had taken it badly but, given the circumstances, the press had forgiven his errant ways. Karin, it would seem, had dealt with her grief by roaming the globe in search of freezing winters or searing summers, skiing in Switzerland or lying on a beach in the south of France, as the youngest Wallis, Emily, completed her studies at boarding school.

The Wallis family's debauched ways had once briefly impinged on Xante—it had been one of his company's boats that the Wallises had died in. It had taken less than five minutes to access their files to find that, in the aftermath of the accident, insurance investigators had questioned the mechanical safety of the boat. His lawyers in turn had accessed the coroner's report and uncovered a few other salient facts, and in no uncertain terms his team had informed the investigators of the boating company's impeccable safety-record. It had also been pointed out that both the boat's occupants' blood and drug-alcohol readings would have rendered a walk in the park dangerous.

Ah, yes; reading between the lines, as Xante always did, Karin's appalling behaviour this morning now made sense. The whole Wallis family had feasted like pigs in a trough on her grandfather's success—had stuffed themselves till the table had lain bare—and still Karin was greedy for more.

Yes, Xante had been irritated and less than impressed as he had sharply rapped on the door to his own suite, eager to get this night over with and to relegate Karin Wallis to the past.

And then he saw her, and again rationale was lost.

Her slender, willowy figure was draped in blush-pink velvet, her pale arms and creamy décolletage mocking, laughing, spitting a hundred times over at the fake-bronze limbs that usually embraced him. She wore no jewellery, except for two diamond studs; she needed nothing else. Her long blonde hair was piled high, sleek and elegant, and all Xante wanted to do was take it down, to unravel it clip by hidden clip.

Kneed in the groin with longing for a moment, all he could do was stay still, to compose himself for a quiet moment as he acknowledged her beauty. He remembered in that moment all that had first captivated him about Karin, and chose to forget their sullied meeting for this one night, to push aside all he knew of her—to just revel in the woman she was.

Walking to the lift, he could feel her tension, despite the cool demeanour. And when his hand located hers Xante expected her to sharply pull away. Instead he was rewarded with the sweet feel of the pressure of her fingers, and then everything changed.

Karin Wallis was his guest this evening, and with every unfolding moment Xante was discovering the difference that made. Her company was engaging, quietly informed; she chatted easily with the most esteemed guest and their partners. And, when the players realised who she was, she was accepted into the fold in a way Xante could never be.

For a while it irked him—it was his hotel, but not his night, and the seating had been arranged so that the players and elite guests were seated at the top table. Only a quiet word must have been had because, with Karin Wallis as his date, suddenly he was sitting amongst the elite now with Karin beside him. Suddenly he was the toast of the table, accepted in a way he never had been before. Still, it was hard to remain irritated with such a rich tapestry of guests, and almost easy to dismiss the part she'd played in his acceptance.

To just enjoy the night, as he had instructed her to do.

Karin declined the wine, taking Xante's word for it that it was excellent, but asking for sparkling mineral-water instead.

'I don't drink.'

'Never?'

'Never.' Karin nodded, accepting her mineral water and blowing out a small breath, realising that she actually was enjoying herself. Oh, she was exquisitely aware of the man sitting beside her, could feel his hand on her arm occasionally, could feel him invade her personal space when he leant over as she spoke—more demonstrative, more expressive, than David had ever been. But here in the bright lights of the ballroom, here surrounded by fellow diners, Karin knew she could keep him at arm's length, and safe in that knowledge she had allowed herself to relax.

'The food is amazing, Xante.'

It was. The roast beef was so tender you could have cut it with a butter knife; trays of roasted vegetables were spread before them, and Yorkshire puddings as fluffy as clouds, which Karin smothered in thick, rich gravy.

'You would not believe the thought that has gone into this menu,' Xante admitted, relieved at the reception of the simple fare. 'I have a very highly strung, but genius French chef—Jacques.'

'Oh?' Karen's fork, laden with very English fare, paused midway to her mouth.

'Last year we hosted the team. The food was superb; Jacques had spent days preparing. I found him in tears the next morning when he found out most of the team had ordered club sandwiches from room service. This year we will make sure no one goes to bed hungry.'

They certainly wouldn't; the sumptuous roast was followed with a selection of puddings—upside-down cake smothered in golden syrup or spotted dick—all washed down with the most delectable custard.

'My grandmother used to make this…' A flood of warm memories bathed her, her cheeks pink as she closed her eyes and took a bite.

'You were close to your grandparents?'

'Oh yes.'

'And your parents?' He shook his head in apology. He knew that he'd crossed the line and was cross with himself that he'd actually forgotten, as they'd dined together, the real reason she was here.

Karen gave a bright smile, and tried to resurrect the conversation. 'Will you go to any of the Six Nation matches next year?'

'One or two, I hope.'

'Surely if they're staying in your hotel…?'

'I am not often here.'

'Oh.'

'I own many hotels—though this one,' Xante admitted, 'is my favourite. But the hotels are only a part of my business.' He chose not to add 'a *small* part', chose not to add that he was the most successful shipping tycoon in modern times and that he employed more people than the hotel staff just to count and track his vast wealth.

'Your parents must be proud.' It was Karin that tipped the conversation into the personal this time.

'My father died when I was nine. In a boating accident.'

'The same as mine,' Karin said. 'More recently, but they died in a boating accident too.'

No; he bit on his tongue rather than say it. His father had died working; his father had been sober; his father had died because the company had sent him out in a badly maintained vessel. It had been *nothing* like Karin's parents' amoral end. Instead of saying it, though, he gave a gracious nod.

'How about your mother?' Karin asked.

'There is only one thing that will make my mother truly proud: it is about this big.' He held his hands a foot or so apart, his smile so devastating Karin found she was smiling too. 'It makes a lot of noise and smells. I am back there next week for a christening. My cousin

Stellios—he is also my best friend—has just acquired one.'

'A smelly, noisy thing?' Karin checked, and Xante nodded.

'So I will suffer the weekend being reminded that I should be settling down with a nice Greek girl and producing babies instead of wasting my time with sport and work and nonsense like that.'

'Do you have many brothers and sisters?'

'Just me.' Xante rolled his eyes.

'Oh dear!' Karin smiled, really starting to enjoy herself now. Xante Rossi up close and personal, apart from being seriously gorgeous, also had this rather dry humour that appealed. 'Well, good luck next weekend.'

There was something on the tip of his tongue—right there on the very tip—the ludicrous suggestion that she come with him. But thankfully formalities took over; the MC stood, the lights dimmed, and Xante breathed out a small sigh of relief.

Since his break-up with Athena, he had never brought a woman back to his island, and if he suddenly were to now the implication would be huge to his family. It had been but a moment of madness, Xante decided. Karin Wallis might have all the attributes of a lady, but under that dress she had a grazed knee where she'd been tripped up stealing. At that moment she leant over to say something, just an observation about the speeches, and Xante caught a scent of her perfume. A stray curl just dusted the edge of his cheek, and he was so lost he had to ask Karin to repeat herself.

The speeches and formalities went on for ever, but neither Karin nor Xante seemed to mind. Sitting together, listening, occasionally talking, they truly appeared a couple. Only, just as Karin truly started to relax, the highlight of the night started—the charity auction. Everything seemed to be auctioned, from Caribbean holidays, a luxurious winter retreat at Lake Como and baubles from Tiffany's that Xante had acquired at a preposterous price for his godchild. And yet all it did was make Karin feel sick. The copious spending, the haemorrhage of money, was all too familiar to her.

But the lavish spending had been just a pale precursor. When the auctioneer silenced the room, the major prize was announced— for a group of up to twenty to train alongside the English rugby team for a week at Twickenham and have access to the top coaches, trainers and masseurs. A headmaster of a grand all-boys school opened the bidding, and Karin watched as the fever in the room mounted. She could feel that there was more than a desire to obtain the ultimate prize— there was the boast of wealth that she abhorred. Like her parents, like Matthew, who'd thrown money away on things they neither wanted nor needed just because it had to be seen that they could. And when Xante trumped the biddings, when the room burst into applause and congratulated him on the obscene amount he had paid for something he would probably never use, Karin was hard pushed to play the part of the dutiful partner and smile at his excess.

That she was less than impressed was blatantly obvious; as Xante pocketed the golden ticket he saw her tongue roll in her cheek.

'You don't seem too pleased.'

'It's not my concern,' Karin said tartly.

'No,' he smiled. 'It's not.'

They sat in tense silence—tense because Xante wasn't the only one realising how much a partner could change one's status. Aware of her Ice Queen reputation, usually Karin stood apart at this sort of function, unable to relax and enjoy herself, rigid and

awkward. It just compounded the rumours.
But just walking in the room tonight she had
felt the shift.

Men had looked at her differently—and
the women too. She was invited into their
circles in a way she had never been before,
moving beyond the awkward, polite small-
talk that was her usual fare, and chatting,
laughing and joking with these acquaint-
ances as if now they were friends, as if now
they wanted to know her.

For a while she hadn't been able to put her
finger on why she was being treated differently. But, staring over at him—dark,
brooding and restless in the chair beside her,
his clean-shaven jaw already dusted with the
shadow of the morning, his hands tapping an
impatient tune with the coaster—Karin got
it. It had nothing to do with her and everything to do with Xante.

Like a rumble of thunder in the distance on
a perfect day, there was this dangerous edge
to him. His sensual lips barely moved, yet
never had a mouth been more expressive.
His body was this ripple of energy and
tension beneath his immaculate suit, and his
eyes when they met hers spoke of sex and sin
and wicked, private places—even if his

words were supremely polite. And if she *were* with Xante, if this night were real, then the newspapers had surely misrepresented her and the company tonight had therefore misinterpreted her—because to be with Xante, to be the woman that held him, meant there was surely more to her than met the eye.

It was with trepidation that she walked to the dance floor with him, as if her awkwardness would reveal their lie.

But awkwardness Xante could deal with. His teenage years had, after all, been spent in a virtual playground of tourists—women out for two weeks of fun and romance in the Greek summer sun, which Xante had been only too happy to provide. He'd driven them on his battered scooter around the islands, their thighs gripping him as the delicious scent of arousal filled the air; he'd taken them to secluded spots, swearing he would write, would ring, that they were the one… So convincing was he that in those moments Xante had almost believed it to be true. It was the chase Xante had relished, the prize of the most unwitting surrender he had sought—and Karin Wallis, tense and rigid in his arms, provided the challenge he had for so long craved. Women these days were just too eager, too ready to please.

But not this woman.

Here on the dimly lit dance floor he held her loosely, feeling her slender, fragile form, his hands low and loose on her waist. He was in no rush. Xante knew exactly what he was doing.

Karin didn't!

All night his eyes had spoken of want, and there had been a raw sexuality to him, this licentious edge that no amount of wealth or trappings could smooth. It had unnerved Karin. Oh, Xante had behaved like the perfect gentleman, and to her surprise he was still doing so now. To her disappointment, perhaps? There was no hint of suggestion in the way he held her; he might as well have been doing a duty-dance with an aunt.

'It shouldn't go on much longer now,' Xante said politely to the top of her head.

'Good,' she said to his chest, yet again there was this surge of disappointment within her that didn't equate with logic. She didn't want him to want her, and yet she did.

His hands on her waist were warm, the subtle scent of him stronger now they were closer, when Karin made her third wish. She wished that this evening were true—that she was the woman who could hold Xante's attention, was the woman that he bedded; that the papers and their rumours were wrong. She knew what the press said about her, knew people thought her frozen and frigid. But beneath that cool surface, that brittle shell, was a woman who yearned to be held and adored, and till now it had proved impossible. Yet here in the darkness, here in his arms, somehow she was able to forget. She felt as if she were dancing on the edge of the sun, that with one false move, one trip, she would fall right in, would dissolve to a delicious nothing.

His hands were just a touch lower now, or maybe she was imagining it. But they seemed to have slipped a delicious fraction, warming her lower back, both little fingers just at the start of the curve of her buttocks. She was supremely aware of her body, only not in the horribly awkward way of before. This was different awareness now; the warmth of his hands spread, this swirl of arousal hung heavy between them. Xante's establishment was way too elegant for something as tacky as a smoke machine, but it was as close as she could come to describing the thick cloak of desire that swirled around them, permeating her skin, her hair, even the air she dragged in. Bubbles fizzed in her veins, little fizzes that buzzed into unfamiliar places. Aware suddenly of her breasts, of their weight peaking in the soft dress, her skin prickling with a need for more contact, low in her stomach she felt an unfamiliar pull, like a string bag tightening. Her body responded as any woman's would, only as Karin's surely mustn't.

She could smell his cologne more strongly now, and as his cheek grazed hers Karin could feel the scratch of new growth just beneath his firm jaw. She felt the subtle nuzzle of his lips in her hair, on her cheeks, and the whispers of breath dusting her ear as his mouth slowly moved towards hers; it would actually be a relief were he to kiss her.

Except he didn't.

Instead he pulled his head back and pinned her with his eyes, told her without a single word *exactly* what he wanted to do, exactly the places he would take her to, if only she might come to his bed. The skin felt raw on her cheeks as it burnt with indecent thoughts, wanting so badly to rest her lips on his, to give in to the subtle pressure of his hands and let their bodies mesh. Except to give in now would mean she must reveal herself later, and the glimpse of disappointment that would surely ensue gave her the strength to hold back, to avert her eyes and loosen his embrace.

He'd almost had her. He'd felt her warm beneath his hands, had seen the naked lust in her eyes, and there had been a rare sense of privilege as he'd witnessed the first stirs of her thaw. But all too soon it had faded. Before the music had ended, he had felt her distance. The lights blazed on, farewells being given, cheeks being proffered and the magic ending. And for Xante the challenge was set.

And it would be a challenge, Xante thought with relish—a challenge that might take a while—but he had never lost one yet.

'I will call you a car.' He watched her rapid blink, knew she was on her guard as she walked swiftly alongside him.

'Xante.' The captain called them as they walked through the foyer. 'Karin… Look, I really *am* sorry about today.'

'Please, don't worry about it.' Karin smiled, remembering, as she always did, her manners. 'If I am going to dash out of fire exits with jewels when the English rugby team are in residence, then I can expect to be tackled.'

'Still. I didn't hurt you?'

'Not at all.'

'Well, I'd like to invite you both to the game next Saturday.'

'Actually…' There was a slight tinge to Karin's cheeks as again, unwittingly, the England captain placed her in a rather awkward spot. 'I'd have loved to—we'd have loved to—but I'm already attending next Saturday's match. They're honouring the game's legends in the pre-match entertainment. I'm to give a speech at the luncheon beforehand.'

'Then we'll have to choose another date. Xante, you said you were going to try to be in London for the England versus Scotland Six Nations match in February; would that suit you both better?'

'We'd be delighted to attend as your guests.' Xante duly smiled, but again he was rattled. Tonight he had chatted with royalty, had sat shoulder to shoulder with the aristocracy, and now had been invited as a private guest by the England captain no less. He had enjoyed every moment. But usually he paid for such privilege. With Karin beside him, it had seemed to be an automatic right—and it *was* vexing.

'It's okay, Xante.' She sensed his discomfort as they walked through the foyer and misinterpreted it. 'I've been to plenty of rugby matches in my time. I'm sure you'll find another blonde to take my place. Anyway I think he'll have more on his mind on the day than worrying where we are.'

'We'll sort something out.' It did briefly enter his head to invite her up for a drink under the guise of collecting her things, but Xante quickly discounted it—he knew what he was doing. 'Let's get you home.'

'Sir…' The night manager was effusive with his apology as they stepped out on the forecourt. 'There may be some delay on the car; all our drivers are taking guests home.'

'Of course.' That had been his instruction, after all; it wouldn't have entered anyone's head that Xante's date for the night might be going home!

It wasn't just the cold air that had Karin shivering as they stood waiting for the car—Karin was waiting for him to pounce, Xante knew, and all it did was make him smile to himself.

He liked making her wait.

'Here's the car now.' Xante was supremely polite. 'Thank you for your company.'

She could scarcely believe he was letting her just walk away—she had tried to steal from him, for heaven's sake! But she had also felt the tension on the dance floor—or at least she *thought* she had. Karin blinked, confused now. 'I can just go?'

'Of course.' He kissed her on the cheek, politely, nicely, and then he stepped back.

The driver was holding the car-door open, and for a moment Karin stood there, non-plussed. 'You'll call?' Karin suddenly said, then checked herself. 'I mean, if you do decide to sell…'

'I doubt I will. Still.' He pulled out a business card and handed it to her. 'You can call and register your interest.'

'You know I'm interested.'

Oh, he knew she was for certain now.

'That is my PA's card—she is very efficient and keeps track of that sort of thing. Maybe give her a ring tomorrow?'

He hadn't even given her his own number.

He couldn't, Karin realised, have made it any more clearer that this *was* goodbye.

'Goodnight, Karin.'

He watched as she climbed into the car.

Women were the only area in Xante's life where he lacked scruples.

Sex, for Xante, was as essential as coffee in the morning, which he liked smooth, strong and sweet. Oh, he treated women well, lavishing his lovers with gifts and holidays and, so rumour had it, he was generous in the bedroom too. But his heart was strictly off limits.

As the car slid off into the night, Xante smiled.

Okay, so tonight he had to sleep alone. But Karin Wallis would soon be in touch and, Xante thought as he headed back in to join the party that was forming in his bar, she'd be well worth the wait.

CHAPTER FOUR

FOR Karin there was no comfort in home.

As the car swept up the drive, Omberley Manor stood elegant, tall and proud. But every light inside was blazing, and even before the driver opened the door and Karin stepped out onto the gravel she could hear the thud of loud music that was ever present at the weekends.

She didn't comment to the driver, of course. Karin had long since learnt that to comment constituted an apology of sorts, and the Wallis family didn't need to do that, didn't need to justify holding a party on a Friday night, to anyone.

Except there was a party at this house most nights.

She pretended to use her key to open the heavy, oak door, but of course it was already open—neither Matthew nor his friends would think of locking it. The house was open to any rich deadbeat who wanted to party till dawn.

Tripping over bodies, bottles lining the surfaces, it was hard for Karin to comprehend that a short while ago she had been dining in splendour, and even harder to face reality.

'They'll go soon,' Matthew said, looking like death as he stumbled along the hallways. His good-looking features had been ravaged from too many years spent living on the wild side.

But Karin knew they wouldn't go.

Friday had already blurred into Saturday, and Karin knew the pattern only too well. Firstly, the apologies that would come on Sunday—or, lately, Monday—and then the massive clean-up that would ensue till the merry-go-round started all over again.

Karin knew it well because she had lived with it all her life.

'They'll be gone in the morning, and then I'll have the place cleaned up.'

It was so pathetic, she laughed. 'They'll go when they've drunk what's left in the cellar and have eaten the food I bought, and have slept in my bed, Matthew.' She clawed at her scalp for a moment. 'I can't live like this.'

'Leave, then,' Matthew said, quickly forgetting to be contrite, his menacing face right in hers now. 'I'm sick of your misery, sick of you embarrassing me, always having a go at my friends. If you hate living here so much, just leave.'

Which was what he wanted.

Which was what, in weaker moments, Karin wanted too—to just walk away and watch from a safe distance as Matthew eventually sold everything off, and the beautiful stately English home that was falling apart at the seams was finally eroded. To just leave and let go as everything her grandfather had built and achieved finally imploded.

Ten months.

She was counting the days, the minutes, till Emily's schooling ended.

Emily was attending the same school Karin had. And, though Karin had long ago worked out that money counted for nothing, she knew only too well the humiliation and bullying Emily would suffer if the Wallises' true status was exposed.

There had already been gentle nudges about the lateness of the school fees; it was the reason she had agreed to auction yet more stuff. Now, if she could just hold on for ten more months, she would tell Emily as gently as she could the truth about their family.

There was a couple in her bed again; the musky smell of excess made her want to gag. Barefoot, she ran down the stairs, ignoring some malodorous comment from one of Matthew's friends sitting on the stairs. His hand caught her bare ankle, his leering mouth repeating his request, and Karin told him exactly where he could go, kicking off his filthy hand and running down the hall, finding the key she kept hidden and heading to the library.

The only place that remained true to her grandfather.

Here, just as she'd done when she was younger, was the place she escaped to. When it had been her grandfather's home, she, her brother and sister would often spend the weekend here. Emily would be tucked up in her cot, Matthew watching television, as their grandmother cooked supper. But Karin had loved the library best. All her grandfather's rugby trophies and medals had been on display, and she had loved to listen to the tales of his glory days, safe and warm and away from the chaos of home.

And, after her grandparents had died and her family had moved in, it was here in the library that Karin had often taken refuge, losing herself in a book rather than facing the reality of what lay outside the door.

She had lived a charmed life, according to the papers—her mother the perfect society wife, a patron of endless good causes and her father a respected member of the bar. Karin had worn the finest clothes and had attended the finest schools. It was the weekends she had dreaded, though.

The weekends when her parents had 'let their hair down'. Weekends when she had tried to amuse Emily and shield her from the grown-ups' goings on.

'Awkward' had been her mother's brittle description of her, and Karin had been aware that she was. So, one weekend when Emily had been at a sleepover at one of her friend's houses, Karin had tried to join in. At seventeen even she had been impressed by the famous actor's charms, had been embarrassed and shy when he had spoken to her, gulping her fruit juice and cringing as the middle-aged man had toyed with her, wishing she could think of some sophisticated, witty retort that might impress him.

It had been an Indian summer, and Karin had felt impossibly hot. She'd been able to hear her mother's laughter coming from the pool and had stumbled outside, hoping the fresh air would clear her head.

And then she had seen her mother topless in the pool and kissing another man.

Despite being appalled, Karin had felt this instant surge of protectiveness for her father, this anger at her mother, and this overwhelming dread that her father might find out.

And then she had seen him.

Had seen her esteemed, respected father fondling another woman's breasts as he'd watched his wife. For Karin, it had felt as if the sky was falling, just a stark, absolute, confirmation of her family's utter depravity.

'Hey!' She could still remember the actor's low drawl in her ear, could still remember the sheer relief of her head on his chest as he had shielded her vision. 'It's okay.'

'It's not!' She had wanted to scream, had wanted to race over to her parents and drag her mother out of the pool by her hair. But she'd let him lead her away, let him take her upstairs, and only then had it dawned on her how drunk she was. Her legs hadn't worked and her head had been spinning—but he hadn't seemed to mind....

Karin couldn't bear to think about what had happened next. Instead, as always, she did her best to look on the bright side. If there was any consolation to be had from the fallout of that appalling time, it was that Karin had, for once, asserted herself. Eight years older than her sister, she had been desperate to protect the nine-year-old Emily, and had demanded of her, for once guilt-laced, mother that Emily become a full-time border at the exclusive school. It hadn't been a complete solution, of course. Emily had often wanted to bring her little friends home, and Karin had always come up with a solution—a holiday invitation from the Wallises was one every little girl craved. So there had been an Easter break in Rome, or the golden beaches of France for summer, or perhaps Christmas in Switzerland.

Life had just been one apparent party when you were a Wallis.

The press were quick to point out that only in the frozen mountains did Karin seem to come alive—printing a beaming photo of her as she'd launched herself off the top of a mountain.

And she had come alive. Away from London and the wreckage of her family, when it was just her, Emily and the crisp white mountains, for a little while she *had* been able to forget. There on the black runs temporary fear replaced constant fear and it felt marvellous.

It had been escape.

A dangerous escape, at times, but at least it had been escape.

Just as her night with Xante had been.

Xante did his level best not to think about her the next morning. Hauling himself out of bed, he showered, dressed and then went down for breakfast, locking the rose back in the display cabinet where it belonged.

He was ravenous, so he pondered the menu instead of her.

He chose pastries and coffee, because that was the Greek way, even though he wanted the full English breakfast.

And he flicked open the paper, fully intending to read about the trouble in the world—except there it was: their chaste kiss as he had said farewell to Karin captured by the press. It seemed ironic for Xante, that for all that he had achieved in his life—all the money that had been raised for charity last night, all the famous women he had dated and bedded—after a single brief kiss with Karin Wallis he was catapulted onto page two.

He did his level best not to think about her in the ensuing week. And perhaps he'd have managed it; had various members of the English rugby team not at various times enquired as to her whereabouts, telling him over and over how delightful and charming she was. Yes, he could have put her right out of his mind—if his PA hadn't rung him to discuss a rather exclusive invitation that had been extended to himself and Miss Karin Wallis: *répondez s'il vous plait*

Only without her, Xante was fast realising, he couldn't.

Still, Xante knew exactly what he was doing. Though it came as no real surprise when on the following Friday Karin rang, the fact she had held out so long meant that there was just a dash of relief there too.

'Rossi.' His PA had already informed him who was on the line, but he let Karin introduce herself and then chatter nervously on for a moment.

'Karin.' He interrupted her attempt at small talk. 'What is it you want?'

'Well, I know you like memorabilia, and I've been going through my grandfather's things, and—'

'You're selling the rest of his stuff?' Xante asked incredulously, though he wasn't really surprised.

'I'm not selling it,' Karin quickly broke in. 'I wondered if you might be interested in an exchange. There are some beautiful things, valuable things. I just really want the rose. I've spoken with Matthew and, even if you were selling it, he's not that keen on buying it back, and all our money's tied up in trust. Without his consent...' Xante rolled his eyes; her sob story he could well do without, but when her voice suddenly broke *then* he listened. 'Xante, please. I really need it. The function co-ordinator at Twickenham just reminded me again that I should bring the jewel; how will it look if I tell them I haven't got it?'

'Like a rather poor effort from his family,' Xante said.

'Quite.' She was crying in earnest now. 'There are trophies, photos; there's even the ball that won—'

'I will pick you up at eleven,' Xante broke in.

'Pick me up?'

'Karin, I have no intention of attending the car-boot sale you are holding.' He examined the nails on his free hand. 'And I have no intention of selling *my* rose. However, I understand your predicament, and I am not leaving for Greece till early Sunday now, so I would be delighted to accompany you. You would hardly expect me to just hand the rose over to you for the day?'

There was the longest pause, but Xante refused to fill it; his final offer was in.

'I'll come to the hotel.' Her voice was strained as she attempted grace. 'But we have to leave at ten-thirty. I have to be there by eleven.'

'You can get there when you like, Karin,' Xante answered coolly. 'I am not available till then.'

He kept her waiting till ten-past.

Then he walked calmly into the foyer where she sat. Karin jumped like a coiled spring when finally he deigned to appear.

But if she was angry at his timing she didn't say it. She kissed him briefly on the cheek and thanked him politely as he handed her the rose. The sobbing woman he had spoken to on the phone yesterday had clearly left the building. Dressed in the palest blue suit, her thick blonde hair for once hanging straight and glossy, she wore a matching coat, the belt loosely tied at the back and her splendid legs accentuated with soft grey stilettos. She looked dressed more for a wedding than for the rugby, and was thoroughly together, mildly bored, even, as she replied in monosyllables to his attempt at chatter when they were in the car. If it had been anyone else, he'd have stopped the car and told her to get out.

It was *his* luxury vehicle they were arriving in, Xante felt like reminding her, *his* rose she was holding, *his* presence that saved her the shame of turning up to the function empty handed, and now she was practically ignoring him. Xante couldn't stand the English obsession with old-versus-new money. Xante knew his worth and was proud of it, proud of his heritage, and proud too that—unlike this polished, groomed beauty who sat tense and rigid in the car beside him—he would never stoop to stealing. Despite a poor upbringing he had made it, without having everything fed to him on a silver spoon and, unlike Karin, he knew how to enjoy himself.

And there was plenty to enjoy. Mingling

with guests, chatting about their mutual passion over a sumptuous luncheon, Xante fitted in well, especially with his prize trophy-date standing beside him. It was the esteemed Karin Wallis who couldn't relax, who shuffled her food around her plate without actually taking more than a single bite. She was excruciatingly polite, of course, and technically never put a well-shod foot wrong. But even as her grandfather's and his team mates' achievements were lauded, even as she took to the microphone, her smile was frozen. Her speech, though well executed, was so lacking in the passion Xante was sure was there beneath the surface.

Only at the end of her speech did she falter, and only then did Xante feel it was the real Karin Wallis speaking

'My grandfather,' she concluded in her prim little voice, 'lived his life just as he played the sport he loved—with passion, flair and dignity. I am not going to distort his memory and say that he would be humbled by today's celebration of his achievements—that was not my grandfather's style. Instead he would have revelled in this day. He would, I know, have loved to be applauded one more time at the ground he called home.'

She returned to her seat to loud applause; applause, Xante realised, that was for her grandfather alone. For that fleeting second he felt he understood her, had glimpsed the pressure of living with and living up to the blaze of glory that surrounded the Wallis name. And when he took her hand and squeezed it, when he told her she had done well, he meant it.

'Thank you.'

She removed her hand and stared fixedly ahead, and Xante held his tongue as another rugby legend took to the microphone.

'Miss Wallis,' an official discreetly spoke when the last of the speeches was over. 'We'll be moving down for the parade now.'

'Parade?' Xante frowned as Karin stood, and so too on instruction did he, and was led through the maze of corridors beneath the stands. Xante was somewhat bewildered but tried not to show it as they were lined up in order, with the elderly greats and their loved ones, or the families of those who were no longer living.

The tunnel was cold and windy. It was a blustery day in London, and gusts swept along the tunnel where they waited for

Karin's turn. To Xante she looked terribly alone.

'Will Mr Rossi be walking out with you?' an official checked, and he knew the answer before it came.

'No. It will just be me.'

The line was moving; each England legend was being announced. Never had Xante felt more of a fool for keeping her waiting in the hotel lobby, and for not knowing just how big and how grand today was for her—and for even considering letting her come without the rose.

'I didn't realise how important today was.' Xante cleared his throat.

'Why else would I have called you?' He could see the flash of tears in her eyes and chose not to take it personally, could see the trouble she was having holding it together as the line moved forward.

'You'll be fine,' Xante said instead, which only confused her more.

Why the hell did he have to suddenly be nice? She knew she was being unfair to him, but it was the only way she could keep from folding. He had no idea what it had taken to ring him, to humiliate herself like that. She had sobbed to him on the phone, and she had never cried to anyone. Around Xante she'd developed the impulse control of a two-year-old. She was freezing; the new designer coat she couldn't afford offered no barrier to the wind, and she felt sick at the thought of going out there, facing the riot of applause and wondering what the crowd would feel if only they knew the truth.

One by one they called the great men's names out, and they or their loved ones stepped out as the crowd roared their approval. Black and white images of their glory days filled the large TV screens around the stadium, and then it was Karin's turn.

As her grandfather was announced the crowd went wild, chanting his name, and Xante saw her hesitate. For a split second he could have sworn she was about to turn heel and run.

'You'll be fine.' He pulled her into his coat, held her for a fraction of a second and kissed the top of her head. Like a father kissing a child on her first day at school, he sent her on her way, and for Xante it was like watching Jonah being swallowed by the whale as she walked out into the ravenous crowd. He had never seen anyone look more little or alone, and even though she was smiling, even though she was waving to the crowd, he knew she was bleeding inside.

What he didn't get, though, was why it should bother him so.

'Karin.' The pre-match entertainment was long since over and they were seated in the stands. The game was underway and still she had barely spoken to him. 'I know today is hard for you.'

'You know, do you?' she sneered. She had to be cruel to him, because otherwise she'd curl into his arms and weep. She had to hold it together for just a little while longer, because there were so many reasons why she couldn't fall apart. 'You could *never* know what today means.'

It had been a thrilling match, worthy of the legends they were honoring. England had roared to victory! But it had been the most appalling date, if you could have called it that. Xante had been merely a commodity, her 'plus one' in every way possible, but he had been too much of a gentleman to just walk. When the last hands had been shaken and she'd declined his offer to come back to the hotel, Xante had dismissed his driver and taken her home himself. As his car crunched on the gravel of her lovely stately home, Karin began to rummage in her bag. For a fleeing moment Xante thought she was maybe going to tip him, but she was only locating her keys.

'Thank you.' She gave him a crisp smile.

She stared up at the house, at the chink of light through the front-lounge curtains. She knew what lay behind them and she didn't want to go in, just wanted to tell Xante to drive on, to just escape.

Xante watched her wrestle with the decision as to whether or not to ask him in, and wondered why she was having so much trouble over just a cup of coffee. She was staring ahead now, still not getting out, her perfect profile rigid, and even when he turned the engine off still she remained seated.

'Are you going to ask me in?'

'No.'

'So why aren't you getting out?'

'You haven't opened the door for me!' It was the most stupid answer—snobby, superior and everything she didn't really feel—except the words just spilled out.

'Allow me,' Xante said. Gentlemen *did* open doors for ladies, but he liked to do things his way, and anyway there was a point to prove. Leaning over, Xante unclipped her belt for her and felt her recoil, pinning herself to the seat, but still she made no move to get out. He knew she wanted him, he could sense it, smell it, taste it, and he knew her head was fighting right now with every other throbbing cell in her body. So what was stopping her?

He leant further over her, flicking a switch so that the door clicked open. A gush of cool night air did nothing to reduce the heat between them. His hair was against her face, his firm body in contact with hers, as way too slowly he moved back. Karin held her breath and could almost feel the ground giving way beneath her; she felt this desire to fall, to just fling herself into the horizon, to just give in. He hadn't returned to his seat; his face turned to hers, nothing but a breath separating them. 'Good night, Karin,' Xante said coolly, still holding her gaze. Karin was mired in conflict. The door was open and she could so easily leave; she wanted this horrible day to be over so that she could walk out of that door and never see him or his vulgar money again. But still she could not move from her seat.

'Why do you fight it so, Karin?'

'Fight what?'

'This.' His lips lightly pressed onto hers and, as much as Karin thrilled to his touch, still she refused to give into his kiss, refused to move as he continued to kiss her.

'Why?' Xante asked, pulling back just a touch, 'Would you fight something so nice?'

He was kissing her again, only less gently now, his tongue parting her lips. It *was* nice, the soft, bruising contact infinitely nicer than anything she had experienced. She could taste whisky and passion—but more than that she tasted the escape his lips promised, lips that soothed and inflamed, that hardened on stirring. And as she kissed him back it was like tripping a switch; this flood of confined energy as his mouth devoured hers was pressing her into the seat; his weight, his strength, was warmly received.

Xante had many kisses in his repertoire; like a skilled magician, they appeared with apparent ease yet were planned and executed to perfection. But not this one.

This was a kiss that even Xante was unfamiliar with. There was no trickery now, no master plan, no voice in his head, just the sweet, sweet sensation of her flesh beneath his.

And then, as her lips parted and his tongue slid inside and met hers, the contact was so shocking that he could feel her tremble. His arms that had been loosely by his sides pulled her into his magical circle, and though he wanted to deepen the kiss he held back, aware at some level that if he moved too fast, too soon, she would disappear for ever.

Only now Karin wanted to stay and wanted to kiss him for ever, because for the first time she forgot.

She was completely and utterly lost in his kiss, and it felt wonderful.

His hands were working down her arms now, as still he kissed her, his fingers stroking her aching nipples through her coat. She wanted them there, only she didn't want them to slip inside, didn't want him to feel the gnarl of the scar beneath. Like the house behind her, the exterior belied what lay within.

He was pressing hard against her and her hands were pulling him closer still, urgent for contact now, not kisses. His mouth was working down her neck as one hand cupped one aching breast, making her stomach curl inside. She felt his other hand wrestle with the buttons of her blouse, and for a second the need for his touch was so urgent, she forgot…forgot… It was heaven to feel his hand slip into her camisole, heaven to rest the weight of her tender breast in his warm palm, heaven till she remembered. Her hand clamped around his, stunned at her own body's reaction, and she refused Xante any more access to her body. Beyond embarrassed, Karin pulled her face away; she could scarcely believe what had taken place.

'Still fighting it?' There was a glint of triumph in his eyes, a look that told her he knew.

'There's nothing to fight.' She gave him a patronising smile, trying to kid them both it had been just a kiss—except it had been so much more. 'I'd better go in. Thank you for your help today.'

'So, I'm dismissed now, I take it?'

'Xante.' She let out an irritated sigh in an attempt to assert control. 'I'm tired. It's been a long day. Thank you for escorting me to the match and for letting me use the rose today.'

'Next time—' Xante started, but Karin interrupted.

'There won't *be* a next time.' Karin spelt it out because she had to, because for ten months more she had promised never to reveal her family's secret. But with Xante sitting so close never had she been closer to doing just that. It was imperative she end this with him right now.

'Next time you'd better make sure you've got a replica rose.' Xante finished his sentence without interruption this time. 'A *passable* fake, one that stands up a little better than its owner to close scrutiny.'

'As I said, thank you for escorting me.' Karin climbed out of the car, his words stinging, desperate to get away from this man who could see through her. But as she finally made to go he caught her wrist.

'You know, when I first met you I *thought* you were a stuck-up ice queen. But now—' he let go of her wrist then '—I *know* that you are.'

CHAPTER FIVE

SHE couldn't go in.

As his car screeched down the drive she leant her head on the heavy front door and couldn't actually force herself to go in to face the chaos that was her life.

She wanted Xante.

All day she had wanted him––only how could she have him?

How could she expose him to the filth that was her home; how could she reveal that the grand surrounds were a sham? How could she expose herself to him?

She wanted to speak with her grandfather too.

Wanted someone to tell her what to do, to hold her up high from the squalor so that she could see the right path to take.

It was easier to get into her car than face it, and as if on autopilot her drive led her back to the place she'd just been. The streets were dark now and Karin put on her lights, her car leading her on the familiar route her grandfather had taken on so many wonderful times in the past, turning onto Twickenham Road and without pause indicating right for Mogden Lane. She had no idea what she would do when she got there, but there was a comfort to be had as she headed along Rugby Road and into Buttercup Lane.

It was almost as if her grandfather was walking beside her as she walked through the near-deserted car park and spoke to one of the night cleaners who thankfully recognised her and let her in. There she sat quietly in the freezing, empty stands, trying to fathom what she should do.

The stands were lit; an army of cleaners moved between the seats, picking up the rubbish, returning the ground to its pristine condition.

Never had she wanted to walk away from her life more, to just give in, because it was hopeless.

'As soon as you believe it's hopeless, it is,' her Grandfather had once told her. She had been a little girl, just four or five years old, but her grandfather had told her the story so many times she truly didn't know if she remembered the day or just her grandfather's recollection of it.

England had been behind. They had lost fifteen out of twenty-three games and had gone into the second half against Ireland 0-3 down. Then the crowd had started singing, Swing Low Sweet Chariot, urging their team on and the dam had burst. England had become unstoppable with the roar of the crowd behind them, storming home to win 35-3.

Only there was no one cheering her on any more, just the weight of it all dragging her down.

Tell Xante.

She could hear her grandfather's voice, and even managed a wry smile at his approval of such an exotic name.

She couldn't. No matter how many times she rehearsed the conversation, she could just imagine those black eyes, narrowing, judging…

'*I have a scar…from a car accident.*'

And then what?

'*I was arrested for drink-driving, but the charges were dropped.*'

'*Oh, and why was that, Karin?*'

There was no bit she could tell without revealing the other—like cancerous seeds, it just spread to every part of her past, to others' pasts, and at what point did you tell? At what point did you trust?

No point.

She clawed at her head.

To tell him some meant she had to tell him all, and she'd tried that once already.

She cringed at the memories, doubled up in her seat and buried her head in her hands. She almost gagged to recall the attempts at love-making with David. David, who had demanded the truth and had reacted furiously when she'd told him her tale. David, who had tried not to wince when she'd shown him her scars and had promised her it would change nothing between them. He had sworn nothing would change how he felt about her, and had sounded so credible—but his body had humiliatingly failed.

Over and over it had failed to respond.

'It's not you,' he'd assured her. Oh, but Karin had known that it was.

'We're locking up, love.'

Karin offered her thanks and headed for her car, turned on the engine and let it sit idling for a moment, trying to think of the bright side—because there was always a bright side, apparently.

At least David hadn't gone to the press. Nothing like a dash of impotence to ensure a man never sold his tale!

She managed a wry smile as she passed the pubs her grandfather had taken her to for many a Sunday lunch, knowing he was watching over her.

Xante wasn't having a good night either.

Okay, he wasn't freezing in the empty stands at Twickenham. But his packed hotel-bar, with the England team enquiring about Karin's whereabouts and asking him to join them offered no comfort. He was restless, angry and frustrated and he headed up to his lavish suite, pacing the floor and wondering what distraction would best suit his volatile mood.

Oh, there were numerous women he could ring. Mandy had left four messages on his voicemail, and there were plenty of others on tap. Even Athena had called, the sound of his ex-fiancé's voice had been a stark reminder, if ever Xante had needed it, that it was right to be suspicious of Karin.

'I am looking forward to seeing you tomorrow, Xante,' Athena had purred into the phone. 'To catching up. To remembering the good times we shared.'

'What good times, Athena?' Xante had mocked. 'You were lying, remember?'

Even five years on it galled him.

He had dated sweet Athena one winter when they'd both been teenagers. He had expertly disposed of the virginity she had been desperate to lose, and they had been a close item. But when spring had sprung Athena had become bored with Xante's grand entrepreneurial plans that took up most of his attention, and had been scathing when he had told her of his dreams. Athena had been innocent enough to think that every future lover would be as skilled as the man who had taken her first, and had headed off on her travels to find a man who had already made it big.

Years later, on one of Xante's trips home, she had *happened* to return too. Of course, Xante had chosen not to tell her of his imminent arrival to the ranks of the seriously wealthy; even his own family hadn't really known just how successful this twenty-five-year-old was about to become. In fact, when they had made love that night on her parents' living-room floor—when she had cried in his arms as to how much she had missed him, how in all the years that had gone by no one had ever come close to him—it had been easy to believe that he was finally in love.

How close she had come to fooling him!

Five years on, still Athena persisted.

The shame, the anger, the humiliation of a wedding that had been called off a week prior to its due date, seemed to dim, and in the past months she had been ringing him more and more. It was usually late at night; sometimes she'd be pleading for another chance, sometimes she'd be bitter and scorning and, at times like tonight, dancing on the edge of seductive.

So restless was Xante that he had even momentarily considered that cold solution, but sweet relief in his native tongue would create its own set of problems.

'Athena, this has to stop...' He'd heard the black silence on the other end of the line. 'It has been a long day and I have to be up early tomorrow.'

'A busy day out with your English rose?' Venom had replaced her seductive tones then. 'I read about you both in the newspaper recently and I watched the two of you together at the game on the television. She does not look much of a match for you, Xante.'

'Still keeping track of me, Athena?' Xante had given a mirthless laugh. 'You would think you would have learnt your lesson by now.'

'Don't you think I have paid for my mistake? Please, Xante, tomorrow you will be home, tomorrow—'

He'd terminated the call.

Tomorrow they would all be watching and waiting for Xante to realise the error of his ways, return to the island and the people he belonged to and claim Athena as his—to restore her honour.

Well, it was no longer Xante's place to do that. He had nothing to feel guilty about where Athena was concerned, and nor where Karin was concerned! He *had* conducted himself with honour; he had bought the rose fairly and had leant it to her for the day, only to be treated like a lackey.

So why the guilt?

Xante often gave away his acquisitions, even returning them sometimes to their rightful owners who had fallen on hard times—so what was different here?

Her.

She had angered him, infuriated him, inflamed him, and then had simply walked away. Karin Wallis was the one woman who had left him feeling used.

Well, no more.

Xante wasn't a rescuer—her troubles, he did not need—yet he did want her. Already doors that previously had been closed to him were opening. He had been invited for lunch this week at an exclusive club, and an offer to join had been extended. His supposed liaison with Karin Wallis had exalted his already high status, and Xante wanted more of the same.

Picking up his phone despite the hour, he informed his PA as to his change of plans, then summoned his driver.

His phone bleeped as the car slid off into the night. 'I need the name of your passenger for clearance.'

'Karin Wallis,' Xante said, snapping off his phone and replacing it in his jacket, feeling the heavy box on the inside pocket of his coat.

There was no doubt in his mind that she'd come. After all, he had something she desperately wanted...

And Karin had something he wanted too.

Exhausted by the time she arrived home, this time Karin made herself go inside.

The house was heaving with the usual occupants, the smell of debauchery in the air, and Karin headed straight for the library, too tired to build a fire but too frozen not to.

Oh, how she wanted Xante.

Bittersweet tears slid down her cheeks, prickles of shame flaring every now and then as to what he must surely think of her. She had treated him appallingly, had been every bit the spoilt ice-queen he had accused her of being—but better that than let him get close.

Wandering around, Karin saw the crystal decanter on the occasional table and, lifting the lid, smelt the whisky and remembered the delicious taste of Xante. For a few moments her body had come alive; for the first time since she had been seventeen she had felt beautiful again, and she *had* been able to forget.

The fire was still too weak for any warmth, the flames just licking the logs, and she stood there shivering, only the memory of his kiss warming her.

And she wanted to taste him again.

Pouring herself a glass of whisky, Karin took a sip, screwing her face as if she were taking medicine. But it was worth it just to remember the taste of him and the reckless, wondrous feel of his mouth on hers. Just as the whisky burnt and warmed her, so too did the memory of his heat pressing into her.

'Karin!' Her brother pounding on the door annoyed her; he had the whole house to mess up, why the hell couldn't they leave her alone?

'What?' Angry, she unlocked the door and opened it.

'Joining the party?' Matthew raised an eyebrow at the unfamiliar sight of his sister with a drink in her hand. 'You have a visitor.'

His head motioned down the hall, and as her gaze followed Karin felt her heart stop. There, standing amidst the debauchery, looking fresh and clean and scathing, was Xante. The contempt in his eyes was palpable as he took in the scene, his black eyes finally coming to rest on her.

'Xante!' Her voice was a croak. 'I wasn't expecting—'

'Clearly.'

She disgusted him.

She stood surrounded by filth, her smart suit crumpled and her face streaked with old make-up, with a glass of whisky in hand, and any trace of guilt he might have felt towards her soon vanished. Feelings of any kind were entirely wasted on her.

She didn't deserve his emotions!

She led him to the library. At least you could see the carpet in here and the air didn't stink of smoke.

He saw her eyes blink rapidly when she saw the box he held in his hand. Blinking to clear the pound signs, Xante thought darkly. She couldn't give a damn about her grandfather. It was all just a game to her, a means to an end, an endless conveyer belt of cash that was slowly winding down.

'Can I get you a drink?' It was the most stupid thing to say, and even as the nervous words came out Karin knew what his response would be.

'Not for me, thank you—but you carry on, though.' Her face was crumpling, and it just enraged him further. He was sick of her tears, sick of her lies and sick of her games.

'I just wanted to taste you again.'

'*Komotakia.*' He grabbed her wrist, disappointment lashing him as his tongue lashed her. 'You lying, filthy lush!'

'It's just a party…' Tears stung her eyes as, despite the irrefutable evidence, she continued to try to hold on to the great Wallis name.

Still trying, as she had as a child, to pretend this was normal.

He stared down at her pretty face and wanted to slap it, wanted to kiss it. He could smell the whisky on her breath and was deranged with disappointment at her lies, abhorring her for not being all that she could be, and loathing himself that he could actually still want her.

Yes; he wanted her.

Wanted her away from this squalor, to see the cool beauty that had breezed into his life return. Oh, he knew he should walk away, just give her the rose and wash his hands of her. Except he wouldn't give her the satisfaction.

He would instead have that sleek beauty on his arm who opened and closed doors, and he would be the toast of London—even if he had to groom her himself—Xante decided.

And he would have her—all of her.

She wanted the rose so badly? Well she could damn well earn it. It was high time to end Athena's and the island's obsession that one day he might return to her. Now, finally, he could put paid to that by attending the family christening with his sweet English rose. A black smile twisted his mouth at the reward that would be his.

'Come,' he ordered. 'You're coming with me.'

'With you?'

'You are coming with me to Greece, this minute.'

'Oh, you want the lush to meet your family now?'

'You *will* be a lady, to them.' Xante's expression was as hard and cold as granite. 'If I have to put you in the bath and wash you myself, or throw coffee down your throat to sober you up. You will be the lady you pretend to be by day, and the woman we both know that you are at night.'

She slapped his cheek then, but Xante remained stony faced.

'Get your passport.' He glanced to the photo of her on the mantelpiece and held it up. 'I am sure it is up to date, what with all your skiing trips.'

'You can't order me about. You don't own me, Xante! You think your money can get you anything…' She was furious and hurting, and wanted him to share her pain. 'Well, it can't.'

'Oh, but I think it can. You see, Karin,

everyone has their price—and I have something you want.' He opened the box he was holding.

She stared at her beloved rose—at Emily's future, glittering and twinkling. It was almost within her grasp, perhaps for the last time ever. The preposterous sum Xante had paid for it, the same sum Matthew had quickly blown, meant she would never be able to afford to buy it back. 'You'd give it to me?'

'You'd earn it.' Xante glowered. 'Every last penny of it. In my bed!'

'That's blackmail.'

'Said the thief!' Xante retorted. 'You're right. I like nice things. But, unlike you, I can afford them, and I can afford you…' He held her pretty chin in his fingers and looked down at her with contempt. 'There will be no more games, Karin.'

'You might get to sleep with me, Xante, but you'll never get to have me!' Karin spat. 'I might share your bed, but don't ever forget you're paying for it the same way that you get to sit with the English rugby team— because you purchase the pleasure of their friendship.' She could see a muscle flickering in his cheek, knew that her words were stinging, and it felt good to shame him as he had just shamed her. 'You line your walls with others people's achievements, but they're not *your* achievements, Xante!'

Xante wasn't open to discussion now, his mind already made up. 'Come; get your passport, get your shoes. My driver is waiting.'

Hell was divided in equal parts by the door, but as he opened it and the sounds of the house reached her Karin knew she couldn't live like this for another minute. Even if Xante was blackmailing her, a few nights in his bed would surely be better than nights shivering in terror on the sofa.

And Emily's future would be secure.

Better the devil you *don't* know, perhaps. Slowly she nodded, opened the dresser and retrieved her passport before heading out to the hallway and putting on her shoes. 'I'll go and pack…'

But Xante wasn't waiting for that. Instead he took her wrist and led her outside as the heavy door closed behind them. As nervous as she was to be with him again, it was over-ridden by a sense of relief. Standing on the stone steps, knowing she wouldn't have to stay there tonight, Karin felt a giddy rush of euphoria. She leant against the door just to get her breath back, closing her eyes, and she could feel the cold night on her face. She was trying not to think about what lay ahead, was just relieved at all she was leaving behind. Karin wanted to get away, wanted time with Xante too—and, yes, she wanted the rose. Except, as a wedge of flesh suddenly pinned her to the door, only then did it truly dawn on her what she was agreeing to.

His kiss reminded her of the power of the man she would be spending the next few days with. His jaw was rough and unshaven, and it dragged at her tender skin. But she was barely aware of it as he moved in closer, his manhood pressing against her serving as a none-too-gentle reminder of all that lay ahead. In his arms, with his mouth on hers, she forgot to be scared. This flame inside licking higher, Karin kissed him back as she had last night, the giddy euphoria of before rushing back in until he pulled his head back. His eyes were black with lust, his mouth full and moist from their kiss, and even as he spoke she wanted him to press his mouth to hers again. But instead he gave her one last chance to change her mind.

'Just so the terms are clear.'

It was to Karin's own shame that she nodded.

CHAPTER SIX

XANTE'S world ran smoothly. Of course, his PA was somewhere in the background, tearing her hair out to ensure such effortless transitions. But within an hour the lights of London were spread out beneath them, and for Karin the truth as to what she'd agreed to was slowly starting to sink in.

Despite her so-called privileged upbringing, it didn't hold a candle to Xante's lavish existence, and the cream leather seats of his private jet did nothing to soothe. Karin was far too aware of the man who sat next to her utterly at ease, his long legs stretched out, chatting into his phone. His suave good looks had never been more daunting, and the sense of euphoria she had felt had long since faded.

This rich playboy, who was used to bedding the most glamorous, sophisticated, experienced of women, thought that she was one of them. But there were no little tricks up her sleeve; her entire sexual *carte du jour* could be summed up in one word: zero.

Maybe she wouldn't have to go through with it, Karin thought, blowing out a long breath, trying to halt the rapid shallow breaths she was taking at the thought of him seeing her body. Maybe one look at her scar and Xante would just hand her the rose and send her on her way.

The thought offered no consolation.

He was still talking away on his phone. Karin knew he was talking about her, but to whom and what about she had no idea. She continued to just stare out of the window as the lights gave way to the black of the English Channel, and the plane lifted higher, along with her heart rate.

Champagne and food were offered, but Karin declined them all. Her eyes felt gritty from too much crying and too little sleep. Yet even when she and Xante were stretched out luxuriously and the cabin lights were dimmed, even when a soft blanket was placed over her by the ever-attentive steward, she still couldn't rest. Xante it seemed was clearly used to grabbing sleep whenever his impossible schedule allowed, and as he rested it gave Karin a chance to look at his features more closely.

God, he was beautiful.

Even in sleep he didn't seem to fully relax. His mouth was closed, his face still scowling, as if at any moment one black eye might peep open and one olive-skinned hand might reach out and grab her.

It was like lying next to a hungry tiger.

Despite the winter month the night air was warm as she stepped out of the plane. 'It never really gets too cool,' Xante explained, 'but this is warm for this time of year. It will be nice if it stays like this for the christening.' There was a luxurious car with driver waiting on the tarmac for them and Xante dealt with the officials as his single case was swiftly loaded. Then they were on their way.

'This is where you live?'

'No.' The sleek car swept through the pre-dawn sky, and Karin put her watch forward two hours, realising that soon it would be morning. 'My family are on another island close by. This—' Xante gave her a thin smile '—is where we will prepare you to meet them.'

'Prepare me?'

'Karin—if we *were* in a serious relationship, if you *were* the woman I had chosen to meet my family—well…' He glanced over to her and frowned, but didn't finish his sentence.

'I don't walk around at home in full makeup and a ball gown, Xante, and I didn't exactly have time to pack and prepare for a romantic weekend in Greece.'

'Which is why we are here,' Xante said as if he were talking to a petulant two-year-old. 'To prepare you. We are staying in a beautiful hotel, with spas and beauty treatments.'

His derision hurt.

She was painfully aware that she wasn't quite up to his exacting standards on every level.

'I'll need to get something. Do the shops open on a Sunday?'

'It's all been taken care of.'

And because it was Xante's world she was living in for now, somehow she knew that it had!

The hotel was beautiful—nothing like the one she had left this morning, but it was stunning all the same. It was way more modern, with glass everywhere, and as she stepped into the foyer only then did his extreme wealth truly start to register. A vast glass display-cabinet stood on prominent display, filled with memorabilia—Olympic medals, a soccer ball. Although it was different from the hotel in Twickenham, clearly it was Xante's hallmark. 'You own this hotel too?'

'Of course!' Xante said. 'I buy friends all over the world.'

His little barb pricked at her conscience. The cruel words she had hurled in their row had been in defence at his scorn. Xante didn't need to buy friends; when he was being nice, his company alone was pleasure enough. But the foyer wasn't exactly the place to rehash things. Instead she walked with him to Reception, feeling like a gypsy beside the sleekly groomed beauty of the receptionist, who flushed just a little and tossed her glossy hair as Xante approached. Karin could feel her rather wide-eyed curiosity and saw a flash of disapproval as, in excellent English, she enquired whether Karin would be requiring the use of the spa in the morning, handing her a huge catalogue of treatments, but Karin declined.

'Maybe a massage to relax you?' Xante suggested. 'They can come to the villa.'

Stripping off was the last thing that would

relax Karin and again, to his irritation, she shook her head.

'Can you at least try and look as if you are enjoying yourself?' Xante said as they walked through the grounds, away from the main hotel. The path was lit, as were the fountains, and everywhere Karin looked there was water—whether it was the black ocean ahead of them, or the steady music of rectangular ponds with fountains that broke the night air. 'You look as if you are here to attend a funeral.'

'Don't worry,' Karin said through gritted teeth, 'I'll turn on the charm when it's required.'

'It is required now!' Xante snapped. 'These people work for me.'

Karin was quite sure the receptionist had already put in a good few hours' overtime; she'd seen the proprietary flash in her eyes when she'd looked at Xante! 'Here.' They arrived at a large whitewashed building. 'This is us.'

It wasn't just the foyer or the gardens that were stunning. As Xante pushed open the villa door and turned on the lights, it took a moment for her head to get round the sight that greeted her tired eyes.

There was a pool in the room!

Not a plunge pool, not a spa, but a large rectangular pool that jutted right out onto the private terrace. At the other end of the room there was a large olive-wood bed that was draped in flimsy fabric that moved with the gentle breeze. Her eyes swirled to the right, taking in the ocean view; the entire end of the room had been left open to reveal its glory. Soft white sofas were everywhere, the rendered, rough walls painted a duck-egg blue, and the whole effect was stunning. If she'd been here for any other reason, this luxurious retreat would have provided a blissful escape.

'This is the honeymoon villa,' Xante explained as Karin's heart sunk further. 'It has exclusive access to a private cove. Come; I will show you.'

'Now?' Karin blinked, but Xante was already heading off.

'We have been cooped up on a plane; it will be nice to get some fresh air.'

As long as fresh air was all that he wanted! She had no idea where he got his energy from. Karin had been nearly twenty four hours without sleep and was wilting like a dandelion that had been mowed along with the grass. Whereas Xante, who had only managed two or maybe three hours at most, seemed as refreshed and invigorated as if he'd just woken after a full eight hours.

Still, the beach *was* beautiful. Dawn was still an hour or so off and the sun was beneath the horizon but awaiting its entrance. Stars were flicking off one by one, as if their owners were heading out, and the black sky had turned to a deep navy. Carrying her shoes, Karin could feel the soft sand beneath her feet, the air cool and refreshing as they walked to the water's edge. Xante didn't bother to roll up his trousers, just waded through it, and Karin did the same. The water was icy, the waves sometimes coming up to mid-calf, but it felt delicious and, yes, it was invigorating.

'Most of the tourists leave at the end of summer; the sun isn't warm enough to give them a tan and they consider the sea too cold to swim in. But I think this is the best time to come.'

'You couldn't swim in it, though.' Karin was shivering just walking in it, but Xante flashed her a strange look.

'I swim in the ocean every morning when I am here.'

'Oh!'

'We grew up by the water; it was our playground all year round.' Xante laughed at her rather crestfallen expression. 'You get used to it once you're in.'

'You must love it here.'

'No,' Xante answered, refusing to be rushed, just strolling along, and it was Karin who had to slow down if she wanted to hear what he said. 'I come to Greece because this is where my mother lives.'

'But it's beautiful!'

'I never said that it wasn't.' Xante shrugged. 'But living here, coming here... The island my family lives on is smaller, it—' He paused, for once his English not coming so easily as he sought the right word. 'I feel closed in; everyone knows your business. It makes me feel...'

'Stifled?' Karin offered, glancing over, not quite comfortable in his company as they walked and talked, but close to it now.

'That is the word! Yes, I feel stifled. I was very clever.' Somehow he said it without sounding pretentious, just stating a fact. 'My parents did not want me to be a fisherman like my father; they had high hopes for their only child. I got good grades at school and I was expected to do law or medicine, then come back and...' He gave a low laugh. 'I don't think I have a very good bedside manner to be a doctor.'

Karin laughed. *In* bed, perhaps, she almost said, but didn't; she was too nervous of what might follow to be suggestive.

'And as for being a lawyer... I cannot really see me sorting out land divisions and deceased's estates. If there was more crime perhaps it would have satisfied.' She could see his point. There was a certain intelligence to him along with this restless energy, and Karin could see that an island, however beautiful, couldn't suffice. 'There is resentment,' Xante admitted. 'I tell you, because you will see it for yourself tomorrow.'

'Because you left?' Karin checked, but Xante didn't answer. A wave caught her by surprise, coming up to her knees, and Karin was buffeted slightly. Xante took her hand to steady her, but she whipped hers away.

'I was just trying to stop you falling, Karin.' The good mood was broken, Xante's annoyance at her jumpiness evident as he turned and headed back for the villa. 'You'll *know* when I am trying to seduce you!'

Which was all very well. But back in the

villa Karin knew that *that* moment was nearing. She wished that she could relax and enjoy the sheer luxury of the facilities, wished she could recapture some of the magic that had caressed them on the dance floor at their first meeting.

A vast showerhead as big as a dinner plate took centre stage in the opulent bathroom, and, having located the switch, Karin gingerly stripped off, feeling horribly exposed and lily-skinned. She caught sight of her scarred, pitted torso and hated herself. There was no juggling of taps to get the temperature right; an instant jet was delivered and she stepped under it, spiky needles of warm water beating her, bidding her to relax, except she couldn't. Washing her body and hair in record time, Karin did try to prepare for what was to come, smothering her body in rich oil and combing through her hair. But, as was her habit, she put her small silk camisole back on and covered her unsightly flesh before pulling on a bathrobe. It was with all the lacklustre spirit of someone preparing to go to the dentist for root-canal surgery that she stepped out of the bathroom.

'Better?' Xante asked as she walked tentatively over to him. She looked about five years younger, with her hair wet and dripping and not a trace of make-up on her face. Bruises of insomnia were evident under her eyes, and so too was her nervousness.

'Karin.' Even the sound of her name made her jump. She was probably sobering up, Xante thought darkly—or coming down. 'You should have a drink, something light to eat.' He gestured to the coffee and juices that had been brought to the villa while she'd showered. The sweet almond pastries just made her stomach curl.

'I'm not hungry.'

'Look.' Xante was losing patience now. 'You ate nothing at the dinner yesterday, nothing on the plane—whisky is not the best source of energy!' His eyes shuttered again, blocking out her earlier explanation, just refusing to go there in his mind. 'You should make the most of your time here—take the spa treatments, eat well, rest.' He wanted that for her, Xante realised. He wanted her to eat nice food and wear nice clothes; he wanted her to spoil herself with treatments in the spa. He wanted her to take care of herself, not for him, but for her. 'Here life is slower,' Xante said carefully. 'Gentler. Maybe it would be good for you to try it.'

She knew what he meant and it touched her that he cared, that, even though he thought the very worst of her, still this imposing man could at times be disarmingly nice.

'Eat.' He pushed a plate of biscuits towards her. '*Kourabiedes,*' he said. 'Like a short-bread. And here, I ordered some hot chocolate for you.'

It was the single nicest thing anyone had done for her in a long time. The jet, the luxury hotel and the promise of the rose all paled beside this seemingly tiny gesture. It had been years, *for ever*, since someone had thought of her in such a way. For ever since her grandparents had put a mug of something sweet and warm in front of her and now, sitting down on the low sofa, it was nice not to examine his actions for a moment. It was even nicer to just dip a biscuit into her drink and pretend that someone actually cared.

'Good?' Xante checked, smiling at her frown at her first taste of Greek hot chocolate. 'They add vanilla.'

'And honey?' Karin checked. 'It's fabulous.' It was. She drained her cup and ate three of the biscuits, but she could feel him watching her, and remembered the real reason that she was here. She knew she couldn't put it off for ever.

Xante watched her slender fingers playing with the scar on her wrist, as he had noticed she did when she was nervous, and couldn't stop himself from asking now.

'What happened there?' Xante picked up her hand and examined the savage scar, so out of place on her soft, smooth skin.

She felt as if he were reading her palm, as if those gypsy eyes could see inside her. Karin snatched back her hand and felt the fleeting good mood between them evaporate again.

'I don't really want to talk about it.'

'You ought to take better care of yourself, Karin.'

'I do.'

'It's time for bed.'

The panic that flittered over her features enraged him. What the hell was she so scared of? He'd felt her unfurl in his arms, and she knew the terms of their arrangement. But a reluctant partner was no partner at all, and Xante wanted her writhing. 'Go to bed; you need to sleep.' He stood her up and practically marched her to the bed. He went to unwrap her gown, but she clung onto it. So he packed her into bed still wearing it, tucking the sheets around her. 'Sleep!' he ordered, because if she didn't take his offer to sleep now, so help him God, she wouldn't for a long time.

It was now Xante who needed a whisky!

He poured a drink and marched out onto the balcony, staring out at the sea, scanning the horizon for answers.

He hated coming back here.

Hated the beach he had stood on waiting for his father to return. Hated the sea that was smooth one minute and ferocious the next. He was dreading the christening, just dreading it, and not just because of Athena. Xante knew he would never walk into that church again without remembering the funeral and the fear of standing beside his wailing mother, this sudden stranger who'd been dressed in black.

Yes, he hated the islands. But most of all he hated the shame and disapproval that was always there in his mother's eyes.

Nothing vindicated him.

Not his money, not his success.

Nothing he did made his mother happy. He had only been half-joking with Karin; a nice Greek girl and gaggle of babies was the only thing his mother wanted, and the one thing Xante refused to provide.

He took a sip of his drink, then remembered Karin's earlier words.

I just wanted to taste you...

In rage and pure frustration, he hurled his glass out to the sea.

How, Xante begged of himself, did she do it?

Did this woman have an answer for everything?

Her eyes were the same colour as the Aegean Sea for a reason, Xante told himself—captivating and inviting one minute, but would ferociously claim a grown man the next.

He sat there staring out at the reddening skies for a long time before he walked over and watched her sleeping. She was curled up into a ball, hanging off the end of the vast bed, defensive even in sleep. Xante couldn't believe the effect she had on him.

He wanted to lean over and kiss her, to wake her up with soft kisses and make love to her. Never had he wanted a woman more—it was the reason she was here, after all—yet he wanted her to want him too.

Stretching out on the bed beside her, still fully dressed, he reached for her and felt her stiffen and tense even in her sleep. He pulled her from the edge towards the centre of the bed then lay and silently watched until finally she relaxed a touch, her dressing gown falling open to reveal the plain camisole beneath. Her damp hair was splayed on the pillows, her face void of make-up. The scent of soap and toothpaste in the air was such a contrast to the scent of glossy beauties he was used to bedding, and never had so little effort been more endearing or confusing.

Enough of this softness, Xante told himself. When they awoke, normal service would be resumed.

But for now she needed to rest…

CHAPTER SEVEN

IF SHE'D had sunglasses handy, she'd have put them on. Waking to the brilliant, dazzling light, it took a moment for Karin to orientate herself.

The clock was nudging nine, and even if she had only slept for a few hours it was still the first proper rest that she'd had in ages—and for once she felt wonderful.

Wrapping her dressing gown tightly around her, she headed out to the terrace to join a very surly Xante, who was reading the paper.

'Thanks for letting me sleep.'

'No problem. Your luggage has arrived.' Xante looked up and gave a tight smile at her frown of confusion. 'I rang ahead on the plane,' he explained. 'If the clothes are not suitable, I can send someone out this morning.'

Her smart new luggage had been unpacked and put away and Karin went and flicked through her new wardrobe. Oh, it was more than suitable; his shopper had thought of everything. The wardrobe was filled with gorgeous dresses, two linen suits, underwear that made her eyes water, skirts, pretty tops, shoes and a couple of pretty camisoles. Suddenly feeling rather guilty, Karin wondered if she got to keep them! There was even a pretty white bikini, which Karin hoped she wouldn't be expected to put on.

Xante had no shame, though.

Dropping his towel, he headed for the pool, and she sat wearily on the bed. Her flimsy gown was wrapped to the neck, and she watched his lithe, toned body doing laps, wondering if he expected her to join him. A knock at the door made her jump, but it was just the waiter arriving with breakfast. Xante carried on swimming. He was so utterly un-inhibited, so Mediterranean, that it only accentuated her English awkwardness. Karin busied herself flicking through her new wardrobe, trying not to think about him so close and so naked, trying to decide what would be best to wear for the christening.

'Don't bother getting dressed yet,' Xante drawled with clear intent, climbing out of the water once the waiter had gone. Dripping wet, he walked towards her and, even though she quickly averted her eyes, it was too late—because one look was enough to tell her he was gorgeous. There was just a small smattering of dark hair on his chest that led a dangerous trail down his body. She'd tried to tear her eyes away, but she'd seen him.

Had seen the thick length of him that awaited her later. Her throat felt impossibly tight, her voice too high for normal. She chatted nonsense about whether one tipped the waiters here, and how nice the breakfast looked; anything other than look down! Without a word of response to her nervous twitter, he picked up a towel and wrapped it around his hips, then headed out to the terrace, where Karin followed.

He motioned to the table, to the spread of yoghurts and fruit, and Karin realised then that she was hungry. Stirring berries into yoghurt, she took a sip of the strongest, sweetest coffee she had ever tasted, and promptly settled for juice.

'So what time is the christening?'

'Two,' Xante answered. 'The hairdresser is coming to fix you at eleven.' Even allowing for poor translation, his words stung. 'Then we will leave at one.'

'It's on another island, though.' Karin frowned. 'Isn't that cutting it a bit fine?'

'They'll wait for us if we are late.' He saw her eyes narrow. 'We are in Greece now, Karin, not London, and as I have already explained things move slower here. Given today is my first morning off in more than three months, I intend to relax.'

Which she assumed meant going back to bed.

'So who's getting christened?' Karin attempted anything to stave things off.

'My friend Stellios—it's his son Christos.'

'And you're the godfather?'

'We've already established that.' He refused to make small talk, to be drawn into her games. Reminding himself what she was here for, he drained his coffee and stood up. 'I'm going to have a shower.' As he walked out of the balcony, he called over his shoulder, 'Feel welcome to join me.'

She couldn't.

She could hear the gush of the water, as the door was left ajar and she sat, trailing her spoon through her yoghurt, feeling sick.

She could never walk in and join him.

Massaging her temples and her forehead now, for once she prayed to get her period, for any excuse, any reprieve…

'Don't tell me.' Xante stood in the doorway, scowling and wet, but thankfully wrapped in a bathrobe. 'You've got a headache.'

'A small one.'

She heard him swear as he dressed, and sat frozen on her seat as he slammed out of the villa. She knew she couldn't put it off for ever.

It was actually very hard work being a playboy's plaything, Karin soon realised.

Even having managed to dodge the morning sex, she still had to look the part of his groomed lover. The thrill of getting her hair and make-up done, just so she was deemed good enough to appear by his side, was fast wearing off.

His mood hadn't improved after his walk, or wherever he'd been. She was dressed and made up now, wearing a pale, lilac linen suit with soft, grey stilettos on her feet. Her hair had been put up, but much more loosely this time, blonde ringlets falling over her eyes. As the hairdresser added the final touches, Xante paced, appalled that his butler hadn't packed his silver cufflinks, completely dismissing the fact that he had given him just two minutes' notice to pack. An angry phone call ensued as some poor islander was no doubt hauled from his bed or the beach to open up shop and rescue the situation.

'I have one white shirt with me,' he said to her raised eyebrows and pursed lips as the hairdresser fussed ever on. 'Do you expect me to be sponsor to Christos with my shirt arms flapping?'

For the first time since they'd landed in Greece, she actually giggled.

'No.'

Silver cufflinks were duly delivered, and as they were leaving Xante picked up a white basket. 'As sponsor, I am supposed to bring certain things.' Even Xante managed a half-smile as he walked out with his basket. 'I know it looks irregular.'

Strange that, as much as she didn't want sex, somehow she still fancied him.

Strange that she was as angry with him as he was with her.

Sparks were flying off both of them as they boarded the luxury boat that would take them to his home island.

'What will I say?' Karin was beside herself with nerves as they left the safety of the villa behind. 'If they ask how long we have been seeing each other?'

'Two, maybe three months.' Xante gave it a second or two's thought. 'That is a long time for me.'

'Wouldn't you have told your family and friends?' Karin asked.

'I do not bore them with my relationships. That I am bringing a partner to a family function is enough.'

'Enough for what?' Karin asked, but Xante didn't answer.

The boat slid through the sea. The waiter brought them over champagne, but Karin declined, requesting instead a glass of mineral water. 'Such a lady,' Xante drawled once her water had been poured and the waiter had bobbed below deck. 'Would you like some whisky with it?'

'Water's fine,' Karin snapped back.

'You don't want to taste me again, then?'

He grinned at her blush, and then thankfully dropped it, explaining a little more about his family. 'Stellios is more than a cousin; we grew up together. I was his *koumbaro*, or best man at his wedding, which means I am now godfather to their first child. It is a big honour. Our families are close, so most of my extended family will be there to celebrate too. Christenings are very important in Greece. My ex-fiancée, Athena, will be there also.' How casually he said it; Karin's eyes jerked up as Xante continued. 'There may be some tension.'

'You could have warned me.'

'I am warning you now.' He gave an easy shrug. 'It was a long time ago; we were engaged for a year.' He really wasn't comfortable discussing this. But forewarned was forearmed, and maybe Karin did need to be aware of a few pertinent facts before he exposed her to the snake pit. 'I called things off a week before the wedding. Our families and friends did not take it too well.'

'A week before?' Karin croaked. 'Why?'

'Because…' Xante flicked his hand as if he were flicking a fly, dismissing the hurt he had surely caused as easily as he would probably dismiss her right now if he knew the truth.

'What about your mother?' Karin swallowed hard before changing the subject. 'I'm assuming that she isn't going to like me?'

'Correct,' Xante said bluntly, then grinned. 'My mother wants me to marry, to give her grandchildren. In Greek families, the mother often lives with the son and his wife. It is natural she would prefer a daughter-in-law that spoke her language, one that was aware of our ways and traditions.'

'It's fortunate for her, then, that this is just a charade,' Karin answered. 'Because I have no intention of ever living with my mother-in-law.'

'Our ways have merit.'

'For you, perhaps.' Karin smarted. 'Two women devoted to your every whim.'

'It is good for the children.' Xante shrugged, infuriating Karin. 'A mother knows best what her son likes to eat, how he likes his food prepared.'

'It's archaic.'

'I agree.'

'I mean...' Karin wasn't listening, warming to her subject, 'What if you want to have a row? What if you want to walk around naked?'

'I said, I agree!' And she realised he had been teasing her; a reluctant smile played on her lips as he continued. 'I just haven't told my mother that yet. So, you want to walk around naked?' She could feel the colour flood her cheeks as he took the glass from her hand.

'I was making a point.'

'You certainly were.' A slow smile curved on his full mouth, the suggestion clear. Karin didn't know where to look, had to fight with her eyes to stay looking at his, despite the burn of her blush. 'You confuse me, Karin,' Xante admitted, except he didn't sound confused at all. In fact, both his voice and actions were assured as he took her hand. 'You tremble like a frightened rabbit, you pretend you are not interested, yet I have seen you watching me.' He took her clenched hand and pressed it against his shirt, splaying out each finger as she sat there burning, trying not to listen, trying to pretend he wasn't reading her mind. He took her un-yielding fingers and slipped them between the button of his shirt, her fingers greeting the warm, silken skin, and then he pressed her hand harder so she could feel the slow thud of his heart. At the touch of his skin, Karin's own heart began fluttering like a trapped bird. 'You were looking at me here.' He pressed her hand harder to his chest, dragging it over his warm skin. 'I know you want me, Karin.'

'Why do I have to want you when I've already agreed you can have me?' Her eyes shone with tears at the cold brutality of their agreement. She held onto her heart because she couldn't give it to him, couldn't let herself admit how much this man moved her.

'You lie even to yourself,' Xante said. 'I would never want a woman who didn't want me.' He was holding her hand, guiding it to his crotch, making quite sure that Karin hadn't misunderstood the *point* she had made. 'You were looking here too.'

'You're disgusting.' She went to pull her hand away, but he held her wrist, his eyes burning into hers.

'You didn't find it so disgusting when you were looking before,' Xante said.

'Someone might come.'

'Don't worry. I pay them well so that they disappear.' She could feel him hard through his trousers, feel him rubbing her hand against him, could feel the power of him. And despite herself there was excitement building inside. Now she looked, looked at her manicured fingers tensed and rigid against the swell of him through his trousers. She could hardly breathe as, still, he stroked her hand against his erection, his eyes boring into the top of her head. Then he removed his hand from hers. If it had been a moment earlier, without the pressure of his hand holding her wrist, she would have pulled instantly away as if burnt. But instead, for a telling time, her hand remained, feeling him of her own accord.

'Any time you're ready, Karin.' His voice mocked her. Her hand felt four times its normal size as it returned to her lap, her palm burning as if branded. 'I'm looking forward to tonight.'

A car was waiting for them, the driver taking them through the streets to a pretty traditional Greek church. Nerves caught up with Karin as she saw the crowd gathered outside, felt every single eye as every head slowly turned towards her.

'Did you tell them you were bringing me?'

'What, and spoil the surprise?'

His hand duly held hers as they approached the wary gathering, and Karin stood with a fixed smile as Xante was warmly greeted.

'Karin?' She heard the question in the voices as Xante briefly introduced her. Thankfully there was no sign of a wronged fiancée, but it was his mother's black eyes that unnerved her the most. Dressed from head to toe in black, she seemed at odds with the buoyant mood, warily accepting her son's embrace, but not even acknowledging Karin. She was much younger than Karin had expected and, though she was dressed in black, there was a modern, vibrant edge to her that defied Xante's rather somber, old-fashioned description.

As they walked into the church, Karin shivered a touch. The weather was good for this time of year, but inside the church it was certainly cool, and Xante's hand suddenly tightened around hers.

She wondered if she'd done something wrong—maybe she had to bow or cross herself, or something—but, turning, she knew somehow his grim expression had nothing to do with her.

'Are you okay?'

'Fine.' It was Xante with the clipped response now, but, though their worlds might be far removed, grief *was* a place she had visited, and Karin instinctively held his hand tighter. She saw the slight frown of surprise on his features but she didn't loosen her grip, and neither did he, till protocol dictated.

As godfather, it seemed Xante had many duties, and he moved to the front of the church, leaving her sitting rigid as the proceedings commenced. Karin was aware of eyes burning into her from the back, and Xante's mother occasionally turning from the front; it was going to be a long afternoon!

'Do you speak any Greek?' A woman slipped into the pew beside her and Karin shook her head, turning gratefully at the sound of the heavily accented English voice. Karin was taken aback by the beauty that greeted her, and knew without introduction who the other woman was. She was stunning. Thick, black hair fell in heavy ringlets, her make-up perfect, her lips painted a vibrant pink, and she was wearing a bright, fuchsia dress that was perfect against her olive skin. 'I'm Athena.' She smiled. 'A friend of the family.'

The service took for ever, but it was very, very beautiful, and Karin was actually grateful for Athena's loose translation of the proceedings. As Karin watched there was a certain pride, a seriousness to Xante, that surprised her.

'He faces west,' Athena quietly explained. 'To the Gate of Hades. Now he stands before the font, the divine womb.' There was so much tradition. The *papas* anointed little Christos with pure olive-oil, and then Xante himself oiled the infant as Athena explained, 'He oils him so that evil slips away.'

Three times the baby was fully immersed, and Karin watched as he was tonsured, his hair cut to form a cross, before being dressed in white.

She felt like a fraud, an unfitting observer at this most intimate, spiritual gathering, but she was enthralled—not just with the proceedings, but observing Xante too.

The ruthless maverick had been left at the door. Now he stood proud, sombre and knowledgeable in his role, fulfilling it with so much more grace than the token effort Karin had made on occasion. At that moment, she was assailed with jealousy, almost—jealous of this family that maintained its traditions, a family that stuck together, a family so far removed from the one she had grown up with.

And then Xante looked over, gave her a smile that wasn't anything other than nice—'a just checking that she was okay' smile—and she burnt in her seat as she smiled back. Felt tears sting her eyes when he looked away. Because she was jealous now of the woman who would one day get Xante. Lucky the woman who would regularly receive that smile, because when he was nice there was no one nicer. Lucky the woman who got to join this fiercely tight circle, and lucky the woman who got to be made love to by that man instead of sleeping with him for dues.

She had only herself to blame for his low opinion of her—and that was what hurt Karin the most.

There was a party back at Stellios's home. The cool air was warmed with *chimineas* as evening crept upon them. A lamb spit slowly turned, and the table was laden with the freshest seafood. It was a feast made in heaven and a day to remember. Karin had one sip of ouzo to be polite as they toasted the baby, and then settled happily back to her water. Xante surprised her again. He was more relaxed than she could ever have imagined, chatting and laughing with family and friends, including her.

The home was lovely, and when Karin went to the bathroom she discovered wedding pictures and family snaps lining the walls. Karin automatically scanned them for Xante, smiling every time she glimpsed him.

As the party moved well into the night, Karin found herself relaxing, sitting back on the cane furniture and smiling when Athena joined her.

'Are you enjoying yourself?'

'Very much.'

'It is a good party. Stellios wanted everything to be perfect for his son.'

'It's all been lovely,' Karin agreed.

'It is funny when you look at Stellios and you see that he is such a family man,' Athena said fondly.

'He seems very proud,' Karin said, struggling just a little with Athena's English.

'Such a proud family man.' Athena gave a fond laugh. 'He was wild when he was younger. Not as bad as Xante, of course… Sorry…' she said, and Karin realised then she undoubtedly wasn't. 'That was not fair of me, bringing up Xante's past.'

'Xante and I have no secrets.' Well, if she was going to play the part of the dutiful girlfriend, she might as well do a damn fine job. Besides, she was curious.

'Of course you don't keep secrets.' Athena smiled. 'I just remember their *kamaki* days.'

'*Kamaki?*'

'Bad boys,' Athena explained. 'Waiting at the airport or at the taverna and watching as the new English girls arrived; they played the game well!'

Karin felt her stomach tighten, knew she was being goaded. But, staring over at Xante, who was dancing, laughing, utterly at ease, she knew it was probably true. A billionaire he might be now, but money and status hadn't fully tamed him; he had that street appeal that attracted women, and those dark good looks that would melt any heart.

After all, it had melted hers.

'I never expected him to end up with an English girl.' Athena's pretty eyes narrowed with spite.

'It sounds like he already has,' Karin said sweetly, refusing to let Athena see she was rattled. 'Several times.'

'Of course.' Athena didn't miss a beat. 'None of those girls ever got it; he was never going to write, as much as he said he loved them. It was just a game, a conquest, one he had to win. That is the thing with Greek boys—they want to claim your heart, want you to love them with passion, and then…' Athena shrugged. 'They leave you weeping. What was it they used to say?' she asked herself, laughing as she came up with the answer. '*Pos boron a echo sevasmo yia mia yinuka an tin gamao*: how can I have respect for a woman if I so easily bed her? Not that it applies to you, of course.' She wasn't even pretending to be nice. 'I'm sure you kept your legs closed for the requisite time it took you to convince him that you were a lady!'

Standing up, she took a slug of her wine, her eyes glittering and dangerous, but still somehow sexy. 'You think you can handle him. Well, you're wrong. There is more to our culture than you can learn. We know our men. That is why...' her smile was black now, her eyes narrowed with malice '...in winter, always they come back to us.'

Xante had told her she should act as if she loved him, after all; if she were here with him legitimately, then how would she handle this? Oh, beneath that icy reserve there was still some fire, and it was a pleasure to ponder— and an even bigger pleasure to react.

'Xante and I are aiming for endless summers.'

'I'm not talking about the weather!' Athena spat.

'Neither am I,' Karin said, remaining seated, eyeing Athena with contempt. 'I wouldn't waste your time waiting for him to come back, Athena; there will be no *winter*.'

'No?' Athena checked. 'Are you quite sure about that? Strange; he was cold and lonely in bed last night after a day with you.' As Karin sat there, cheeks burning with humiliation, Athena continued, 'I don't have to be beside him to keep him warm, Karin. Home, after all, is only a phone call away.'

It was lucky she was sitting down, Karin thought as Athena flounced off; her legs were shaking from the confrontation, her head buzzing with images she didn't want to think about.

'Trouble?' Karin almost jumped out of her skin as Xante's mother sat beside her. Bracing herself for another verbal lashing, Karin was surprised that after an afternoon and evening of black, suspicious looks Despina had come to make peace. 'That girl is trouble.' She gave Karin a warm smile; she really was a stunning-looking woman. 'I see you help him in the church; still that place upsets him. It is good to see him happy tonight. So many times at these things he stands apart…'

Xante was enjoying himself.

Family things were usually fraught, but not this one. He hated going to the church, but today being with Karin had made it easier, and tonight he had actually kicked back and relaxed. He had enjoyed catching up with Stellios and his cousins. Karin wasn't one of those needy women; just as she had at the hotel, she had chatted and mingled readily, despite the language barrier.

Glancing over, he had seen Athena talking to Karin, and though it should have unsettled him—he knew what Athena could be like—Xante hadn't been worried. From Karin's poise, the way she had handled herself in the church, he was quite sure she was a match for Athena. Anyway, he was paying her well!

So, for the first time in family history, Xante relaxed and partied into the night.

Till he saw her talking to his mother.

Xante was over in a trice to help Karin out…

Only his mother was not only smiling—worse than that, she was laughing.

'The party is finished…' She was even talking in English! 'Now you bring Karin home.'

Karin didn't really understand what was said next, the word *'Mykonos'* was bandied about a few times, and she was fast learning that *ochee* must mean 'no', because Xante shook his head every time he said it. Eventually she understood that, here in Greece, Despina ruled.

'We're staying the night at my mother's.' Xante's face was like thunder, as he took her hand. She could feel the tension in it as they bid their farewells, laughing to herself, almost; this was so not how he had planned it.

It was a short walk to his family home, up another cobbled street, and Despina let them in to the unlocked house, leading them into a lounge Karin assumed was kept for 'best', because it was spotless. All her needlepoint was proudly on display, and little crosses and candles surrounded pictures of what could only be Xante's father.

'She likes you.' Xante gave a slow eye-roll as Despina went off to the kitchen to make coffee.

'Sorry about that.' Karin smirked.

'Everybody likes you!' Xante brooded.

'Not everyone,' Karin said brightly. 'I don't think I'm much of a hit with Athena. I thought she was your ex.'

'She is!' Xante said.

'Yet she still *rings* you?' Karin's eyes narrowed; she could feel this lick of jealousy curling in her stomach that wasn't actually merited. It was none of her business what Xante got up to, and Xante told her as much.

'*Had* we been seeing each other for two months, that question would be merited.'

'You really can't live without sex, can you?' Karin sneered.

'Why would anyone want to?' His question made her burn, as did his raw, brazen sexuality she envied so. 'Why, Karin?'

'Because it should mean something,' Karin croaked.

And for that he had no answer, because in that Xante was fast finding out she was right. Xante was tired of snapping his fingers for service, tired of rolling over in bed and trying to remember her name, tired of being three months into a relationship and finding out she bored him. He stared over at Karin's pale beauty, at the one woman he couldn't win on charm alone, a woman he had to bribe to get into his bed—a thief, a drunk and a liar.

And yet there was a dignity to her that captivated him.

His mother was calling out to him from the kitchen, but it was Karin's eyes that blocked everything out. Karin was a woman with whom sex would mean something.

Despina was nothing like the suspicious woman from the church. She sat, laughed and chatted, and showed Karin hundreds of photos—including a curly-haired little girl whom Karin could have sworn had horns!

'Trouble!' Despina said, tapping the photo.

'I thought you were on Athena's side,' Xante reminded her. 'Last time I was home, you were still hoping I'd see sense and marry her!'

'That was a year ago, Xante!' Karin was touched that in front of her they spoke in English, even when the conversation was uncomfortable and it would have been much easier to revert to their native tongue. 'Things change in a year—not that you'd know!'

'I've been busy.'

'Always busy!' Despina rolled her eyes, then looked over to Karin. 'I hope he has more time for you.'

There was no right answer, so Karin didn't offer one. For once she just sat, watching Xante, who was looking less than comfortable as his mother continued. 'Athena likes a lot of this…' She rolled her fingers and thumbs together in a cash gesture. 'And I hear in the village that she likes a lot of this too…' Despina pointed down to her crutch, shocking Karin but making Xante give a snort of laughter. 'The two things *you* are good at providing,' she said, pointing at Xante.

'You will see that my mother doesn't mince her words.' Xante grinned at Karin's taken-aback expression. 'Here in Greece, we say it as it is.'

'You certainly do!'

'Watch her, Xante,' Despina warned. 'She makes trouble.'

'We were finished five years ago.'

'Athena doesn't think so.'

There was the customary viewing of the house before bedtime, and when Despina pushed open a door and gestured to a single bed Karin could have kissed her.

'You sleep here, *kalinihta*.'

She glared at her son in a stern warning, and Karin hardly dared looked at him— except she couldn't resist. His petulant face, like a cat thrown out in a storm, really was a sight for sore eyes.

'*Kalinihta,*' Karin said sweetly, giving him a kiss on the cheek and closing the bedroom door. For the second night in a row, rather than earning her stripes Karin slept beautifully, encased in crisp, white cotton, with Despina no doubt guarding the door.

CHAPTER EIGHT

WAKING up in his mother's home—hearing the bustle of the kitchen, smelling the scent of coffee, pastry and almonds, and Xante and his mother chatting in their native tongue—for the first time in the longest time Karin realised she had overslept.

The single bed was so cosy and warm, the house so welcoming, the voices wafting through the walls so soothing. It was tempting to just roll over and go back to sleep and pretend that this was all real, that this was her life, but of course it wasn't. Instead, Karin showered and dressed. Last night's suit seemed a touch over the top for breakfast, so she left off the jacket and wore bare feet before heading out to her unlikely host.

'*Kalimera!*' She smiled to Despina as she walked into the kitchen, then to Xante, who was sitting reading a paper at the table. She kissed his unshaven, scowling face. 'How did you sleep, darling?'

'Better than I will tonight!' Xante warned. She could taste salt on her tongue as she licked her lips.

'Have you been swimming?'

'I told you, I swim in the sea every morning when I am here.' Xante returned to his paper. 'It was rather necessary this morning, though; I have to work off my energy somehow.'

'Poor Xante!' Karin answered, realising she was still smiling—had been smiling, in fact, from the second she'd awoken. Two nights away from her brother and the chaos at home, and she was starting to relax.

Really relax.

She had been right to get away; that little bit of distance was helping her to see things more clearly.

She was tired of the facade, tired of trying to keep the once great Wallis name unsullied. She was also tired of lying for Matthew, and even though it had never been Xante's intention this tiny escape had been more than a reprieve—it had been her salvation.

'Not quite how you planned it, is it?' she said softly, not mocking him now.

He caught her eyes, gave her a very be-grudging smile, and then another one—a dif-ferent smile this time, ironic and funny, and it made her smile too.

And though Karin wouldn't want to live with her, even if it came with the bonus of Xante, Despina really was delightful. This busy, elegant woman with shrewd eyes and sharp wit was a wonderful host, and could easily shock and make her laugh.

Xante was certainly his mother's son.

'I tell him to take you to mountain. His moped is here.'

'You have a moped?'

'All Greek boys have mopeds…' Xante rolled his eyes. 'It's ancient. I doubt it will even start, let alone get us up a mountain.'

But his cousin still used it, apparently. And, anticipating arguments, Despina had found a cream crocheted-cardigan and a pair of pretty flat shoes for Karin. Xante's shirt looked okay rolled up, minus the silver cuff-links, but he refused point blank to wear an old jumper of his father's. And, to Karin's nervous surprise, an hour after breakfast Despina had packed a lunch and a blanket and was waving them off. There was no hint or suggestion of a helmet. They probably weren't going that fast, Karin consoled herself, yet it felt like it, buzzing along the hillside, her skirt pushed up more than she would like, the wind whipping her hair, the winter weather so mild it could almost count as an English summer.

Feeling his muscles beneath her fingers, the air growing colder as he took them higher, she could feel tiny goose bumps on her skin. Then, when they bumped off the road and onto a beaten track, Karin had no choice but to wrap her arms around him if she wanted to stay on. The moped bumped her forward and her cheek brushed his back; it just felt right to rest her cheek there now, right to hold on tight and sink into him.

There was a strange feeling of déjà vu for Xante as the forest sped by. He felt her knees avoid gripping him at first, then felt her slowly give in, her hands now holding tight around his waist. Up the mountain they went past all his regular haunts, and for Xante it was like reliving his past.

But it was *there*, as her arms finally wrapped around him, that any *déjà vu* ended. There was no rush of triumph as he felt her lean into him, no unseen smirk on his face as he felt her body finally yield. His throat was so tight he could hardly get air in; he felt hollowed out with a sudden gratefulness as finally she accepted him. There was no fire in his groin as he raced now to bed her, just a need, a want to hold onto this moment for ever, to ride on and on with her soft body warming his. Xante truly didn't know where he was going. He knew the mountains like the back of his hands, but he just didn't know where this was leading.

He took her to a small copse, laid the rug on the ground, and they ate bathed in green, bosky light, his black eyes trying to work this elusive woman out. Her hair was tangled from the ride, her eyes clear and bright, and if he'd had a camera he'd have captured her image for ever. She was the most beautiful woman he'd ever seen, carefree and laughing.

Lunch was simple but fantastic, great chunks of bread which they dipped in olive oil; a crisp Greek salad all washed down with a bottle of sparkling water.

And for the first time ever, he told someone.

Told her how it nearly killed him to come back home.

How he hated the island and the waters

that had taken his father, and most of all how he hated the company whose negligence had caused it. How, at nine years old, he had sworn revenge and had worked his fingers to the bone to achieve it.

'I bought the company when I was 22.' Xante was lying on his side, propped up on his elbow, while Karin lay on her back staring up at the tree tops and wishing she never had to go home. 'And then I sacked every corrupt manager who worked there. I paid the fishermen properly, repaired their vessels so they were fit to go onto the water… It all grew from there. Now I can support my mother properly—not that she wants it. She is happy to live in the house she lived in with my father. For her, money changes nothing. She will wear black till she dies.'

'She seems happy.'

Xante shook his head.

'She does!' Karin insisted, but she could see his point. This beautiful, vibrant woman, with so much love to share, was alone in the world. It didn't seem fair. 'How old was your father when he died?'

'Thirty.' Xante didn't elaborate, but there was a pensive note to the single word that had Karin catch a breath for a second before she spoke.

'The same age as you are now?'

'You are twenty-five, yes?' Xante checked, and Karin nodded. 'My mother had me when she was sixteen. Her life was over at the age you are now.'

'Not over,' Karin croaked, but his words were so close to the bone it hurt. They weren't talking about children, grandchildren, careers and houses, they were talking about sex, love, passion and romance. Talking about the very thing that, prior to Xante, she had been sure she would have to forever live without. 'You should try to come back more often,' Karin pushed, even if it wasn't her place to.

'So I can watch her grieve? So I can listen to her tell me again how I always let her down?' Xante shook his head 'I caused her a lot of pain in the past…' His face was grim.

'She seems to have got over Athena.'

'It's not just that. I was wild as a teenager, angry with the world; I caused her shame.'

'Teenagers often do,' Karin said softly. 'They push the boundaries, rebel against everything, and then hopefully they live long enough to grow out of it.'

Why did she have to say the right thing and make him feel better? He'd never shared like this, never opened up to anyone—and he wasn't sure he liked it.

'What about you?' Xante asked. 'What were you like as a teenager?'

'I don't know...' Despite the cool air, Karin felt impossibly warm. She reached for the bottle of water and took a drink she didn't want. 'Quiet, I guess—rather boring, really.'

'No teenage dramas?'

Karin gave a tight shake of her head. 'I was too busy studying for there to be any drama.'

'Did you go to university?'

'No.' She could feel the colour whoosh up her cheeks, could almost feel the implication. She'd had the best schooling and the best opportunities, and she was still just an assistant at the library where she'd worked a Saturday job as a schoolgirl. 'I didn't do as well as expected in my exams.'

'And if you had?' Xante pushed. 'If you could be anything you want to be...?'

Why did that question make her want to cry? Because she'd never even asked it of herself— not once in all these years had she allowed herself the luxury of a future that was hers.

'I'm happy as I am,' Karin said instead,

except there was a hollow note to her voice that she couldn't quite smother.

'And your army boyfriend?' He watched as her shoulders stiffened. 'What happened there?'

'What happened with you and Athena?' Karin challenged, sure that would silence his questions, but after a moment's hesitation Xante answered.

'I found out the sweet girl that had pined for me all those years was actually cunning and manipulative. She had set her sights on me and my wealth.' He watched Karin's eyes widen at his admission. 'We went out when I was just a fisher boy, and Athena wanted more from life. She travelled Europe, and we did not see each other for many years. I started to do well. As I said, I bought the company... only I never really said just how well I was doing. Athena returned from her travels and said she was thrilled to see me, told me she had always missed me. She didn't even know I had bought the company or how rapidly it had expanded...or so she let me believe.' Xante's black eyes met hers. 'A week before the wedding, I found out otherwise. She had known all along about my success and had set out to become the type of woman she believed

I wanted—she played the part very well. I ended it when I found out.'

'How did you find out?'

'Athena had confided in a friend from the day she had set her sights on me. She told this friend of her intention to marry me and live a wealthy, comfortable life. A week before the wedding, that jealous friend forwarded all of Athena's emails on to me.'

'You didn't tell your family what you knew?' Karin asked.

Xante shook his head.

'Why?'

'Because…' He gave an exasperated shrug. 'It is hard to explain. I took her virginity. We were a couple, we were engaged, we wore rings. For Athena, there would always be the stigma…she was going to remain here. But it was easy for me, who had no intention of staying once I found out the truth.'

'And now?'

'Now, she gets maudlin some nights. She rings and tries to rekindle what it turns out we never had. I tell her no.' He looked her in the eyes as he said it, and Karin actually believed him. 'We have been over for a long time— Athena just has to get used to the idea.'

'And that's why I'm here?'

It was part of the reason she was here, Xante reminded himself. Only why was he talking to her; why was he telling her things that no one else knew? Why did this woman move him? 'So what about you?' Xante said, annoyed at his own revelation. 'What happened with you and your handsome captain?'

Karin thought for a long moment as to how to answer, but when it came the answer was surprisingly easy.

'Same as Athena—I wasn't the woman I appeared to be either. And, like you, David couldn't deal with that.'

'You're nothing like Athena.'

'No?' Karin challenged.

'No,' Xante said, shaking his head. 'Because away from it all, when you forget you're supposed to be a bitch, it turns out you're actually a nice person. Talk to me, Karin.'

'Why?' Angry eyes met his. 'I'm not here to talk, remember?'

'Maybe I want to get to know you.'

'Maybe you wouldn't like what you found out.' She held her breath, scared how close she was to revelation, but also scared of his reaction. Because how could Xante believe she didn't have another agenda, that her appalling finances had nothing to do with her feelings for him?

Feelings.

The admission came like a slap. There were feelings, real, solid feelings, which she had known were there all along. Because without feelings she would have never agreed to this. 'Maybe if you knew the truth it would ruin things.'

'You're right.' He thought about it for a moment then said it again. 'You're right.' He ran a hand along the curve of her waist, reminded himself again of the real reason she was here. 'It took me a while to get over Athena, but she did me a favour. Love is for fools, Karin. Always there is an agenda; always it is not as it seems.'

'Not always…' She could feel tears running down the back of her nose, because she didn't want it to be so. She still wanted to believe that love could, did, always win in the end; she was arguing with herself more than him. 'Look at your parents; they were in love.'

'So you are left a fool, or you are left living a life in mourning.' He shook his head, his the voice of reason. 'It is better this way.

This way—where we both know what we want, where there are advantages for both of us. And no one needs to get hurt.'

Except she was hurting already.

Missing him already, because surely soon he would be gone.

Since Xante had come into her life, it had changed. Somehow, despite the poor image he had of her, she had felt looked after. When trouble had come, she had someone she could call for the first time since her grandparents.

That day at Twickenham, she had felt safe with him by her side—and she felt safe now. Safe enough to kiss him. She *had* to kiss him, not because he demanded it, but because she wanted it too and very soon, she would.

She wanted to know what it felt like to be in the arms of a passionate man, to be held and caressed and made love to, before truth stepped in and claimed her. She wanted to just hold onto this moment for as long as she could, so she might take it out again at a future date and replay it.

He was stretched out beside her, still propped on his elbow, and as he reached to get his drink his shirt lifted, offering Karin a glimpse of his flat, toned stomach, of a snake of black hair…and this time Karin didn't avert her eyes.

This time, Xante didn't make a smart comment when he caught her looking.

'I don't bite.' His voice was thick with lust, the air still and silent, and there was nowhere to hide. But this time Karin didn't want to.

'Promise.'

He pulled her towards him, his mouth on hers exquisite. His face was cold, his warm tongue rolling around hers, capturing it, sucking on it, and she could have kissed him like this for ever. Except kisses couldn't last for ever, at least not a kiss as good as this one. He was pulling at her top, but she moved his hands away, instead sliding off his shirt, feeling the satin of his skin beneath her palms. He rolled her onto her back and, kneeling up, he straddled her, still kissing her as he did so, trapping her with his knees, his hands holding her wrists loosely above her head, just kissing her till she craved more contact, till her body was squirming beneath him. Her hips rose but he wouldn't relent, just confined her in the delicious space that he had created, and tormented her so with his mouth till she could take it no more and she was rewarded with his full weight. Her skirt was up around her waist, his erection pressing hard into her groin, stroking her through his trousers. Karin stroked him back, the motion of her hips involuntary as she rubbed into him. He slid her panties down, and she could feel the cool air between her legs, then warm, patient fingers stroked her so slowly that for just a second she forgot and entered this gorgeous sweet place where it was only them. A place not sullied or tainted where her body was hers, and his was his, to do with what they would.

His other hand was moving to her blouse again, wrestling it from her waistband, and she knew Xante wanted her naked. It was for other reasons that she pushed him away this time. Now she wanted the moment that had eluded her for so long. She grappled with his heavy leather belt, her trembling fingers wrestling with the buckle, and then finally she held the delicious, strong length.

For Xante her tender exploration was more than he could take, his erection so fierce that he knelt up on his heels, holding her hips in his hands and even the short distance seemed too long now. He didn't understand her. She was pleading with him to go on, purring his name, begging her demands. Yet her eyes were wide and he could feel an intimate resistance as he entered that had Xante in heady ecstasy. With each measured thrust she gripped him tightly; it was a case of one step forward and two steps back, and then he was in, and he just melted deep in to her. Since the first time he had laid eyes on Karin, she had consumed him—and now he consumed her.

For Karin, it was heaven.

Those shallow, first thrusts slowly beckoning her closer.

His maleness pressed on top of her, inside her; the sheer relief of a body that worked, that this man who had made her a woman, was swelling and bucking inside her.

She could feel his abandonment, feel this powerful man temporarily lose control, and she lost it too and gave in to a sensation that ripped through her body. A decadent rush of feeling shot from her spine to her scalp, made her thighs convulse, and took her head to a place where red was all she could see and skin all she could feel. Feel the rapid friction of him against her, the greedy pull of her centre as it accepted every precious drop. This frantic, urgent coupling taking place for

Xante bought a heady relief, but there was a thud as he came down. Holding her in his arms, he stared up at the tree tops, running a hand along her goose-bumped arm. Xante could feel the thick flesh of the scar on her wrist, only he wasn't feeling it idly.

For the first time, as he lay replete on the mountain with a woman in his arms, still there was more from her he wanted.

More, Xante was sure, than Karin would ever give.

CHAPTER NINE

THE Greek sun, even thin and weak in winter, still worked its magic.

He watched the tension slowly seep out of her. There was a pale smatter of freckles that had appeared on her upper thigh, Xante saw as she dozed on the day-bed beside him, wearing the white bikini he had bought her, but with a sheer-turquoise shirt tied around her midriff. A heavy, hand-crafted silver Byzantium bangle he had bought her when they had come down from the mountains and wandered through the village shops of his home town rested on her wrist, covering the scar he knew was there. Her creamy cleavage spilled out of the bikini top, the only ripe flesh on her lean slender body—yet Karin seemed to hate it, keeping herself covered when Xante wanted to see all of her.

They had returned to the villa and had stayed on for an extra couple of nights.

Karin slept a lot, ate fresh, good food, and walked on the beach every day.

The Aegean Sea was for once to Xante beautiful, still and peaceful as the sky turned orange. Yet it was Karin he was watching now, and wondering why the sex between them hadn't rid his system of this woman.

Xante's body tightened in recall at their love-making—which was what it had been; sex was such an inadequate word to describe the places they had taken each other to. But, despite the closeness, always Karin held back, always she left him wanting more.

Maybe in three months he'd become bored with her, Xante tried to tell himself.

Maybe in three months' time he'd find that plummy accent grating, or her chaste ways irritating.

He wanted more from her.

He wanted an open door on the shower, and for her to swim naked in his pool. He wanted her to revel in the body she seemed so ashamed off, and he wanted more of her than he'd ever wanted from any other woman. Certainly more than Karin was prepared to give.

They were flying out in a couple of hours. Evening was creeping up too soon, and for all his power Xante realised how little he really had. Night would fall and dawn would follow, his plane would lift off at seven and by midnight it would all be over.

Which was as it should be.

Emotions confused things. Relationships should be treated like a good business transaction, Xante reminded himself—mutually beneficial—which this was. Their whirlwind romance was still making the papers. Xante Rossi, the fisher boy from Greece, was finally accepted as one of the English elite. His in-boxes were full of new contacts, new invites, a whole new world for him to enter— and Karin would have the rose back.

He should be delighted how things had turned out.

He *was* delighted, Xante told himself.

Only why, for the first time in years, did he suddenly want to stay in Greece for a while longer?

He was stroking the curve of her waist, just idly exploring the contours without really thinking, his fingers tracing the dip and then the rise to the curve of her hips. It was only when she moved a touch that Xante consciously realised he was touching her. Relaxed in sleep, she'd never been more beautiful, her body stirring at his tender command, as if in her dreams she was waiting for him to join her.

In that lovely place between sleep and wake it was so easy for Karin not to think about tomorrow, and the next day, and the future without Xante; so easy to just lie here and let his hands bathe her body. She had come alive in the last few days; with his skilled attention, Xante had taught her just how natural and beautiful love-making could be. She knew it would soon be over, knew this was to Xante, essentially a business transaction—yet it was so much more to Karin. Her body was awash with the first peace it had felt in years, a body that worked—and it was Xante who had revealed it, had brought her in closer contact with herself than she ever could have imagined.

Karin knew she was right not to tell him about her past. She didn't want sympathy in the bedroom, didn't want to share her pain, and she certainly didn't want to reveal her financial predicament to the man who was waiting for her to do the very same.

And she didn't want to say goodbye, but that was how it had to be.

He was stroking her stomach now so lightly; his touch was barely there, but she felt the ripples build inside so exquisitely. Her bikini was damp with arousal, her nipples like thimbles, so tender that just the weight of the fabric on them hurt. She didn't want to open her eyes; all she wanted to do was feel. His other hand was lifting her hair; his breath was on her neck as still he stroked her, his mouth massaging the tender skin where her neck met her collar bone, his hand creeping inside her bikini bottom, stroking her sweet, warm place. Slowly his mouth continued to work down, kissing the top of her cleavage, and she wanted him so badly to take her breast in his mouth, except… Her head was thrashing with indecision; she was warm and pliant in his hands, but there was a frantic calculation going on in her head as to where her scar was, how much she could reveal without revealing it all. There was this ache for him to take her nipple in his mouth as his fingers slipped inside her top, his palm giving heavy attention to her breast as his mouth moved down.

It was her right breast, Karin told herself,

the scar was the furthest from that one. And she squeezed her eyes closed as he moved the flimsy fabric just enough to accommodate her desires. Her hand was on high alert to halt him if he moved her blouse any further as her mind contracted to the delicious focus of his mouth nearing her tender peak. She was watching now, dizzy with desire, his fingers sliding deep within as first he licked her swollen nipple then he blew softly, doing it again and again till it begged to be kissed—which he did. She watched as those beautiful lips now worked her swollen flesh, sucking it, toying with it, teasing it till she wanted to weep in his mouth and come in his hand. Except his desirous mouth was moving again, his free hand toying with the tie of her shirt. But Karin knew she couldn't let him, could almost see the shock that would surely end this delicious exploration.

'Xante.'

She pushed him back, saw the blaze of confusion in his eyes.

'Karin, I want to do these things.'

'No.' It was such a simple word, and for Xante a powerful one too. She could say no and mean it, didn't have to justify or explain, because this wasn't a relationship where you gave and took and worked on things; this was business. Karin was torn between want, need and shame, and she kissed him fiercely, straddling him as he pulled at the ties of her bikini bottoms. She sank onto him, crying out as he filled her with this contrary blizzard of feelings, because Xante demanded so much more of her than it was safe to give. He was holding her hips, angry almost as he ground into her, giving her what she wanted when he wanted to give her so much more.

His fingers were digging into her buttocks, his hips lifting off the bed, and he could see her breast free from its confines, wet where he had kissed her. He pulled her down and his mouth claimed it again, sucking hard as he pounded inside her and she could feel his confusion and anger. Karin was angry too, angry at a past that sullied the present, angry for all that she would leave behind tomorrow. She could be angry and that was okay; it felt wonderful. And he could be angry too, and still he could make her feel safe.

She could hear the moans and the tension, hear them hasten, and she wanted to watch him this one final time. Lifting her head, her breast wet and cold, she stared down at his beautiful face and black, angry eyes—she hated him, too, hated him for making her feel, for showing her just how good it could be. She was crying as she came, crying, because it was such a relief to feel, such a relief to go to dangerous places and have Xante beside her, inside her, to watch him come. She saw the pained look of pure pleasure on his face as still she came, weeping in sweet relief when finally it was over, because it hurt to give so much to this man, and it was actually a relief that soon it would end.

Afterwards, as he lay beside her, Xante had no idea what had happened. He tried to fathom what had taken place. Because there was sex, and there was sex, but with Karin it was always different. If there was a line, then somehow they had not just crossed it but had taken a leap to the other side, and there was no going back.

'Karin.' He actually had to clear his throat to drag some power back into his lungs. 'Why won't you…?'

'Leave it, Xante.' In one movement, she climbed off the bed.

'You don't even know what I was going to say.'

'I don't need to.'

'When we make love…'

'We have sex, Xante,' Karin corrected. 'That was the deal, remember? Sex for the rose, and I think I've kept up my end of the arrangement.'

'Karin!' He called her back as she headed for the bathroom. 'What is it you are hiding?'

'That's none of your business, Xante.' She was so close to telling him it actually scared her. She needed to get back to London, back to reality, so she could remind herself again why she couldn't open up to him.

'What if I want it to be my business?'

'I'm a thief, Xante. No!' She shouted the word when he opened his mouth to interrupt her. 'Sex—that was what we agreed. My feelings aren't up for sale.'

'You're no whore.' He was off the bed now, catching her wrist as she turned for the bathroom. '*That* had nothing to do with the rose.'

She took back her wrist. 'I'm not some tourist, *kamaki* boy; you don't have to make me fall in love with you to get what you want from me. You don't have to bleat out promises you have no intention of keeping. We had a deal. Now, if you're not satisfied with the service, then I'll give you a quick one on the plane as an added bonus. But apart from that I think we're done.'

A filthy mouth didn't suit her but then, Xante reminded himself as she slammed into the bathroom, the Karin he loved didn't actually exist.

Loved.

He almost spat as the word came to mind.

The woman he wanted was just an illusion.

As they headed out to meet the driver, Xante handed her a set of keys and the safety-deposit box address. They were both bristling with rancour, and the holiday was clearly over.

'I won't take you up on your charming offer,' Xante said as he helped her into the car. 'I don't have to pay for sex.'

Even if it hurt, even if this was agony, surely it was better to keep him out rather than let him in? Taking the keys, she slipped them in to her purse and made it exceptionally clear that they were over.

'You just did.'

He didn't ring her, and neither had Karin expected him to after their bitter parting.

He didn't text and neither did he email, and she knew that because she checked both her mobile and computer regularly.

There were no flowers to follow. Apart from a new set of keys on her key ring, and a heavy silver bangle which she never took off, there was no proof that anything had actually happened between them.

But there were changes.

No matter the circumstances of their arrangement, or the fact that it had never been his intention, Xante had empowered her. That small reprieve from her life, that small glimpse of being treated well and cared for, had made Karin realise that the unbearable was actually impossible.

That ten more months might just as well be ten more years; she couldn't, wouldn't, live like this for a moment longer.

Sitting at work, entering the late returns into the computer, Karin was trying and failing not to think about the lunchtime appointment with her lawyer.

Her lawyer.

Not an old friend of her father, or a contact he had once fostered.

Just a reputable name from the phone book, and hopefully a step in the right direction.

'We have a problem.'

She didn't look up, just blinked as her two worlds collided. Xante's rich voice, too loud in the library, his scent replacing the musky book-smell. The beautiful hand that had touched her so intimately came into view as he handed her a thick white envelope.

'We've been invited to attend a ball.' He waited while she read the invitation—a royal invitation—which of course demanded a prompt response. Which of course, Karin told herself, was the only reason he was here.

'There is no *we*.'

'We were in yesterday's newspaper,' Xante pointed out, and finally she looked up at him. Looked into his eyes for the first time since they had made love, looked at that haughty, sexy, slightly depraved face. And she never wanted to look away. 'Did you read about our *honeymoon* in Greece?'

'No,' Karin lied, dragging her eyes away from his and returning to the computer screen.

'I'd like to accept the invitation.'

'Then accept.' Karin shrugged, tapping away and inadvertently deleting outstanding fines. 'Pretend I'm sick on the night, or that we've just broken up; that's not such a bad idea, actually…' She gave a tight smile. 'You might just manage to buy yourself a title!'

'It's you they want,' Xante said, because it was the truth. 'It's you *I* want,' he said, because that was the truth too. In the week since they'd returned, he hadn't been able to think straight, and had slept alone each night for the first time in sixteen years. He didn't understand what was happening, except that something was, and that something had to be dealt with. He watched her fingers as they paused over the keyboard and knew his admission had shocked her as much as it had shocked him.

'I'm busy that night.'

'What about tonight?' Xante pushed. 'We could go for dinner.'

'It won't just be dinner.'

'I won't lay a finger on you,' Xante said, and two old ladies peered over their magazines and gave each other a nudge. 'I just want to talk.'

Her cheeks were as red as if he'd slapped her on both sides of her face. She wanted him to go, but she wanted him to stay. 'What if there are things I don't want to talk about?'

'Then say,' Xante said. 'We will talk about movies and books and what your fa-

vourite colour is; we will start at the begin-
ning as if it were our first date, as if we
never slept together.'

'Shh…' She knew everyone was listening.
He was just so big and loud, and even his
whispering filled the silent building.

'I promise not to have sex with you,' Xante
whispered loudly, and somehow that made
her smile. 'I promise not to kiss you or even
hold your hand. I promise only boring,
superficial conversation…'

And it did sound tempting, because she
actually wanted to tell him. And maybe, just
maybe, she would. Oh, not the whole lot, of
course—but maybe she could come to the
table tonight, having seen her lawyer, and
could tell him about her scars and explain
why she could never show him. She didn't
have to tell him the whole sorry story
because Xante had taught her that she could
say no. Could say 'no, I don't want to talk
about it yet'; it was like having been handed
the golden key. She could feel herself tipping
into trust and it felt as if she were falling,
taking this leap into the unknown and
praying inside that he might be there to catch
her. 'Dinner.' She gave a sharp nod of her
head. 'Just dinner.'

'I'll pick you up at eight.'

And then she had to sit in a library that was watching her and pretend that life was normal, that the man who had just left hadn't walked out holding her heart in his hands. Karin had to wait till her coffee break when no one was listening to ring and book herself in for a blow dry for five. And even in her race to get to the lawyer, even with Xante's promise of no sex, she was ten minutes late for her appointment—because a pretty lacy cami with matching panties just called to her from a window… The underwear was wrapped in tissue paper, placed in a box and into a pretty bag, and she held onto the pink, ropey handles like a security blanket.

For the first time ever she sat through the gruelling hour with *her* lawyer, and told someone about *her* past, and started to plan *her* life.

It just somehow felt nicer in the knowledge that tonight she would be seeing Xante.

Delighted with himself, Xante waltzed through the foyer of his hotel, but groaned somewhat when he checked his messages. That little jaunt to the library with his phone off had cost him dearly.

But Karin was worth every penny.

'Athena.' Xante deliberately kept the surprise from his voice as his ex-bride-to-be approached him in the foyer. 'What brings you to London?'

'The shops!' Athena smiled. 'Then I realised how close I was to your hotel and I thought it would be nice if you took me to dinner.'

'You should have called me,' Xante pointed out. 'Unfortunately my whole day is already taken for, and I have plans for dinner tonight.'

'Of course; I know how busy you are.' Athena's smile stayed intact. 'But surely there is time for coffee? I would hate to go back and tell everyone that you did not have time for an old friend…'

'Of course,' Xante smiled. 'There is always time for coffee with a friend.'

Seated at the table, Xante gave the orders, his mannerisms smooth, belying the unease he felt. Eternally vigilant, he was never more so now, positive that Athena hadn't been 'just passing'. Playing the game all the same, he listened as she rattled off her purchases, which luckily didn't take too long.

'Your mother seemed very impressed with

Karin.' Athena wasted no time getting to the real reason she was here.

'Karin is an impressive woman.'

'I am worried, Xante.'

'Don't waste your energy worrying about me, Athena. I can take care of myself.'

'I know that—I know better than most that you look out for yourself.'

'I looked out for you too, Athena,' Xante pointed out. 'I could have told everyone about your plans, showed them your emails, and no one would have blamed me for what I did.'

'I am not talking about that, Xante. No; it is your mother I am worried for.'

'I look out for my mother too.'

'You have hurt her in the past, though, and not just with our break-up.' Athena's eyes met his, watched the grim set of his jaw, the slight swallow that told her he was rattled. 'But with your careless ways…'

'Athena!' Xante was tired of playing games. 'What is it you have come here to say?'

'Your mother's excited, naturally. Karin is the first woman you have brought home. Already she is talking marriage. You know she is desperate for you to give her grandchildren.'

'It is early days for me and Karin.' Xante was annoyed now, seriously so. His mother liking Karin so much had come as a surprise, and he certainly wasn't looking forward to hurting her if things didn't work out between them, but it was none of Athena's business. His mind flitted as it often did to Karin, to the woman who was slowly working her way into his heart, and when he spoke it was the truth. 'I will never marry or have children just to keep my mother happy—but, yes, Karin is a very special woman.'

'What do you know about her?'

'Everything I need to.' Xante drained his coffee. "Athena, I think I have heard enough; I am busy.'

'Fine.' Athena stood up and went through the ritual of kissing him on the cheeks before she offered her parting shot. 'If you are not worried about her criminal history, then you're right—I have no need to be. I am sure you have everything under control.'

'Criminal…' Xante shook his head. 'Look, Athena, there was a misunderstanding the other day.'

'The other day?' Athena's almond eyes narrowed. 'I have no idea what you're talking about, Xante; obviously she makes a habit of acquainting herself with the police.'

'Athena, we all have pasts.'

'Sure.' Athena shrugged. 'But drunken assault?' She watched a muscle pounding in his cheek and knew that she had him, knew this was news to him. 'Of course, it must have been a misunderstanding; the charges were dropped once the victim had been discharged from hospital. Either that, or it was one of the benefits of having a very rich daddy to help you out!'

'How would you know this?'

'Friends in the right places,' Athena retorted. 'The same as your girlfriend.'

She was wrong, Xante told himself, hating himself for doing it, but consoling himself he was proving her innocence as he scoured the Net. Her name was everywhere, but there was nothing that confirmed what Athena had said. He scoured images, the news, and with every article that his frantic eyes scanned his heart beat slower. He felt confident enough now to click on his phone and ring Paulo, a private detective who did some occasional work for him.

'Karin Wallis…' He felt like the biggest

rat in the world, but he so badly wanted Athena to be wrong. She *had* to be wrong. Karin wasn't just any woman; she was this woman who was under his skin, in his heart, constantly on his mind. This was the woman he could so easily give his heart to, the woman who might even one day be the mother of his children. 'I can't find anything on the Net, but the charges were dropped, apparently.'

'Leave it with me.'

He didn't want to leave it with him.

He didn't want the truth.

Giving his driver the night off, he drove to her house, knowing he would see her soon; ignorance was very nice, thank you very much.

His phone was bleeping, alerting him to a text as his tyres hit the gravel of her driveway, but Xante ignored it.

There was a vast skip that didn't seem to belong outside such a stunning home filled with bottles and garbage bags, and he could hear music pumping from the house. Just then his phone rang.

'I can't get much.' Paulo was apologetic. 'There wasn't an official gag-order, more a gentleman's-code-of-honour thing…'

'That's fine,' Xante said. 'Thank you.'

'There are a couple of articles. I'll send them over now—just local papers, but they've all been pulled.'

'Don't bother.' He wanted ignorance. He could see the curtain twitching, knew that she was waiting for him, and that was all he needed to know.

'I can get Reece to dig deeper; he knows some of the journalists in the area.'

'Let it go,' Xante said, only Paulo wasn't listening; he was reading off his list, because to him Karin Wallis was just a name.

'She's in debt up to her eyeballs. It's going to come down like a pack of cards soon. It's all there—drink-driving, assault, suicide attempt, rehab; the usual stuff.'

And, when you asked for the truth, what right did you have to complain if you didn't like it?

Xante stared at his phone and watched as reams of texts appeared: scattered articles, photos, her debts, the loans, her credit-rating; the whole sorry lot was there. At every turn he'd listened to his heart rather than his head. Over and over he had accepted her excuse as well as making his own for her. He had wanted so badly to believe in her, but at every turn he had been thwarted.

Xante had cried once, the morning his father's body had been discovered.

Twenty-one years later, he did so again.

CHAPTER TEN

SHE was ready and waiting, wearing a smart grey-wool dress and with her hair down, a coat of blonde around her shoulders. Xante stood in the hall as she picked up her coat, trying to return her smile as she looked around for her keys. The thumping music was messing with his head.

Karin was messing with his head too.

'You were sitting outside for ages.'

'I had to make a call.'

She frowned at his glassy eyes. 'Are you okay?'

'Great.'

'Sorry about the noise,' she said, raising her eyes to the ceiling; the lights literally shook with each thud. 'Still, I won't have to put up with it for much longer.' She gave him a bright smile, closing the door, and followed him out to the car.

There was a brightness to her Xante hadn't seen before, and usually he would have found it appealing—but not tonight. He was tired of the many faces of Karin, and tired of trying to work her out.

Tonight he *would* get answers.

Her brightness soon evaporated; she could feel his mood smother her like a cloak. A strained, one-sided conversation took place between them on the short drive to the restaurant, Karin dragging out 'yes' or 'no' answers from her clearly reluctant date.

The rain was falling so fast the wipers couldn't keep up with it, but Karin thought she'd rather be out there, somehow, than stuck with Xante like this. She could see his tense profile as he reverse-parked, fitting his luxurious car into an impossibly tight spot, and suddenly Karin just didn't want to do this. She was too tired for games, and had enough pride in herself not to sit through a strained dinner just to have him dump her at the end.

This was supposed to be a date, not a summons.

'You know, suddenly I'm not hungry.'

'The table's booked.'

She was having great difficulty trying not

to cry, but she absolutely refused to. 'Look, clearly you don't want to be here, and guess what? Neither do I. So can you please just drive me home?'

'You don't want to know what's wrong?'

'You're thirty years old, Xante!' Karin said. 'I shouldn't have to guess at it. If there's something wrong, then I assume you're old enough to tell me yourself.'

'Here.' He pulled out his phone, scrolled through a few texts and handed it her.

And as she stared at her past, she lost what she'd started to believe might be her future.

'You've been checking up on me?'

'It's the only way I can find anything out about you. You're not exactly forthcoming…' He gave up trying to justify it; he knew that he probably couldn't. He had told himself over and over on the drive to the restaurant, not to push it, to drop it, to leave it— except he couldn't do that either. Her little dig about being out of the house soon had tightened the already-taut coil. 'When were you going to tell me, Karin? Once we were safely married? Once you'd got what you wanted?'

'Once I trusted you,' Karin broke in, handing him back the phone and stepping out into the driving rain. For a second she popped her head back in. 'Which can never happen now.'

She knew he wouldn't leave it there and she was right.

Like a kerb crawler he drove beside her to the house, window down, shouting at her to get in, but she didn't look over at him and she didn't answer—because if she did her response certainly wouldn't have been ladylike. She wanted to spit, swear and kick at him, but instead she ran. Racing up the stone stairs of her home, she tried to brush past him as he jumped out of the car and raced after her, but he wouldn't let her go. 'I just want some answers. Karin, I just want to know what's happened to you.'

'To check whether I'm suitable?'

'Yes!' Xante roared, because it was the truth. This, the woman he wanted as his wife, the woman who would, God permitting, be the mother of his babies.

'Well, it doesn't matter any more,' Karin shouted. 'Because, after what you just did, *you're* not suitable for *me*.'

She hated him, and she hated his opinion of her more. She was so tired of the lies and the secrets, and if he wanted to know so badly then she'd tell him—she'd serve up her pain and see if he enjoyed tasting it.

Putting the key in the door, she opened it. She didn't invite him in, but didn't shut him out either. If Xante needed answers, he could have them.

And then he could leave!

She took him into the library, because it was the only decent room left in the house.

Dripping wet but ever the lady, except for the times she forgot to be, she offered him a drink, but Xante declined.

She had been rushed into this moment, but she refused to be rushed any more. She took her time to light the fire, trying to work out what she would say to him.

It had been disastrous when she'd told David.

His horror and anger had been everything she hadn't needed. Her tears had only made things worse, her emotion inflaming his. She was determined not to repeat it with Xante.

The balled newspapers shot smoky flames that licked at the logs. The central heating had long since given up the ghost; she was shivering wet, but Karin knew it would take for ever to get warm. Once this was over and Xante was gone, she'd have a nice, hot bath and get changed.

Once Xante was gone… Her head tightened at her future, because he would be gone and he'd have lost *them* for ever. The second he had handed her that phone, he'd snapped them into the past tense.

Now she just wanted it to be over.

'The only truly great Wallis was my grandfather. The only thing my parents were good at was partying, and my brother Matthew is just the same. That party you witnessed the other night wasn't a one-off, it happens all the time. The only decent thing in this family is my sister Emily. The rose will help to pay off her final school-fees and hopefully get her through medical school.

'We're broke,' she said flatly.

'It doesn't stop you jetting about,' Xante pointed out.

'Better that than bring Emily back here.' Karin shrugged as if it were easy. 'Better that than expose her to what I had to put up with. It's all a facade, Xante, and one I had intended to keep up till she finished her schooling—except I can't. I can't live like this for a moment longer. All I want is a quiet life; that's all I've ever wanted.'

Xante shook his head. 'Don't try to tell me again that you were boring as a child, don't tell me again how you like to lock yourself in here and just read, that you never drink. You were arrested for drink-driving!'

'I *was* arrested.' Karin's voice was matter-of-fact. 'When I regained consciousness from the car accident, there were two officers by my bed and I was charged with drink-driving and causing actual bodily harm. My father arranged it so that the charges were dropped— which saved him the discomfort of explaining the wild party that had been taking place in his home, and that one of his closest friends and most prestigious guests had attacked his seventeen-year-old daughter. It also hid the glaring fact that both of my parents had been too passed out or stoned to do anything about it, and saved them from having to explain how they didn't even find out about everything till the next day.' There, she'd said it, and she hadn't been bitter or angry, just felt relief.

The pain she'd once tried to spare him was all there on his face. 'You were attacked?'

'Yes.' Clear, unblinking eyes stared back at him. 'Obviously, it never went to court;

my parents were worried about how it would look.' Only then did her face flicker. 'I *was* drunk—because my drinks had been spiked. I know that, because I was seventeen and, unlike my parents, I obeyed the rules and had been drinking orange juice. I started to feel sick and I remember being led upstairs to my room. He'd always seemed such a nice man—well, what I'd seen of him on the television. I honestly thought that he was helping me, and then...' Karin sucked in a long breath. 'Well, I'll spare you the details. But as drunk as I was I did try to stop him. I smashed him in the face with a glass I grabbed from the bedside.'

He watched as her fingers automatically stroked the scar on her wrist.

'I cut myself in the process. So, you see, it wasn't a suicide attempt.' So coolly she read his mind. 'At the time, I actually thought I was saving my life.'

'Karin, you don't have to say anything more...' He was appalled, sick to his stomach at what she'd been through, and at her treatment at his hands too. He wanted her to stop, wanted to take her in his arms and tell her he was sorry, so sorry. But Karin didn't want to hear it.

'I'm tired of covering up for my poor excuse of a family. I'm tired of staying locked in the closet with their skeletons. You wanted the truth? Well, now you'll sit and hear it. After it happened, I drove my car to get away from him, from them—from this hell hole. I was trying to get to the hospital to get some help, except I smashed the car on the way.'

Xante reached for her arm, trying to comfort her.

'Don't!' Spitting with anger, she stood, all the pain, grief, shame, and rot that she had stuffed down all the years propelling her from her seat. Her usually pale face was red with fury. 'You had to push. You just had to keep working away till you got your precious answers! Well, here they are—I did drink and drive, and our family is in debt. But your precious source got one thing wrong—I didn't go to rehab. That was my mother. She felt so guilty that she managed to sober up for a full three months!'

'Karin—'

'Terrible, isn't it?' Karin snapped. 'Terrible to have to sit and listen to all this. But it's worse being the one to remember it. It damaged me, Xante, and it took me years to even *start* to trust someone else, years to have a relationship. David was a nice guy, nice enough that after a while I was able to tell him part of what had happened. He was a nice enough man to take it slowly, and to say that the scars on my chest wouldn't turn him off if I showed him…' A scream was boiling inside her, gushing up, and she didn't know how to stop it. This rip of pain was shooting from her lips, and hardest of all for Xante was that he'd lost the right to comfort her. He knew that if he so much as touched her she'd hit him. His punishment now was to sit and listen to her pain and be unable to do anything to alleviate it. 'Except they did turn him off. They turned him off me!'

'Karin, I didn't know.'

'Well, now you do!'

'Let me help you.'

'Help me?' She let out an angry wail that was almost a laugh. 'I *was* going to tell you; I *was* starting to trust you.' She jabbed a finger in his direction. 'You walk around like a Greek god with your perfect morals, your exacting standards—but only as far as they suit you…' She was ranting like a deranged woman, but she didn't care. Boy, it felt so good not to care and to speak her mind. 'You collect trophies and claim them as your own. My grandfather bled for that rose. He lived, breathed and slept rugby—he gave everything to represent his country. He worked two jobs and still turned up for training every day. You… You wave your money around and just buy everything, the same way you bought me. And now suddenly I'm not good enough? Well, guess what? I don't want to be your token blonde, Xante. I don't want to be on display for others to admire, a little trinket to add to your collection.'

'You're not.'

'I was.'

'No.' Of that he *was* certain. 'Karin, at every turn I wanted to believe in you. You're angry with me because I'm not supposed to care about your past. Except I do care—I care about you.'

Karin just stood there, drained from revelation and too bloodied to fight any more, to even think. 'Just go.'

She'd dreaded his pity, but if anything Xante was actually angry at her. 'Don't sit there on your high horse, telling me I dragged the truth from you. I had every right to know that truth when I slept with you.'

'It was easier for me that you didn't.' There

was a first twitch of guilt as Xante got straight to the brutal point.

'Well, it wasn't easier for me,' Xante answered. 'I should have known that, Karin. What?' He demanded to her shuttered face. 'I'm not allowed to be worried about you, not allowed to be confused by your actions? I'm not allowed to care?'

'Just go *kamaki* boy.' She watched him wince, but she just wanted him gone. Wanted to be back on her moral high-ground, because it felt so much better there. 'Go back to your hotel. I'm sure there'll be another nice girl to add to your collection. One who's not quite as hard work as me!'

He did turn to go, but he changed his mind.

'For your information, I didn't make a very good *kamaki* boy. I adored every one of those women; every one of those women, I hoped I might learn to love…' His black eyes found hers. 'Eventually I did.'

'Just get out.'

She was actually glad when he did.

CHAPTER ELEVEN

EVEN before the black row with Xante, Karin had made up her mind.

'Grandfather wanted the house to stay in the family…' Matthew was immutable when she told him her plans the next day—and insisted they were carried out too.

'He wanted a lot of things,' Karin retorted. 'This house will be sold, whether it's by us or the banks. Matthew, we can't afford it any longer.'

'We can sell some stuff off.' Matthew shrugged. 'The library's full of first editions; those gloomy paintings—'

'If we sell the house,' Karin interrupted, 'We can afford to keep some of those things. We can both start again.'

'It will be bought by developers.' Matthew tried to hit her where he knew it would hurt, only he didn't realise that she was beyond pain now. 'It will be turned into a hotel, with weddings held here every week. You said yourself it would be a tragic waste if that happened.'

'There's been plenty of tragic waste in this family,' Karin said. 'Let's just finish the job.'

Matthew was the first to leave the sinking ship, moving in with friends to carry on with his partying ways, leaving the hard work for Karin.

She'd expected nothing less. In fact, Karin was glad of the solitude. Cleaning up the house, dealing with estate agents, ringing up creditors and explaining the situation felt cathartic. And with every call, with every passing day, she knew she was doing the right thing.

The heady Wallis days were over. They had, in fact, been over long ago; her family had just refused to let the party end.

Sitting on the veranda with his mother watching the New Year fireworks light up Mykonos in the distance, the *chiminea* and ouzo keeping them warm, Xante knew he had been right to come and spend Christmas and New Year with his mother and to try and make peace. He just wished that Karin were here too, as did Despina.

His mother had been disappointed at the news of his break-up with Karin, and disappointed with him too. Xante had given her a rather heavily edited version as to what had occurred, and his mother had reminded him that she had warned him Athena was trouble.

That always he rushed in, demanding action and answers.

Always he was sure he knew best!

Xante had conceded all points, and now they sat in slightly strained silence as Xante worked up to make an apology that, in his mind, was long overdue.

'I'm sorry.' Xante turned to his mother and said what was on his mind. 'Sorry for all I put you through those times.'

'What times?'

'My *kamaki* days.'

'Oh, Xante.' To his bemusement, she laughed. 'That was years ago.'

'I caused you shame when you didn't need it.'

'Xante, you were a teenager. You are my son; I forgave you even as I beat you.' She laughed at the memory of chasing a gangly teenager around the lounge with a belt.

'You were so upset…'

'Of course; I didn't want to be a Grandmother. How times change! Xante, I was upset about a lot of things at that time. I was in mourning.'

'You still are.'

'No.' She shook her head.

'You will always wear black.'

'I wore black then to show I was grieving. I wear it now so that I remember—there is a difference. Every morning I dress for your father, I am happy. Xante, you can stop worrying about me.'

Xante looked into his mother's black, merry eyes and realised that Karin had been right. For the first time he realised how necessary it had been to come here—not to make family peace, but to make his own peace. 'You are the one in mourning,' Despina said.

'Yes.' Xante nodded, because there was no better word to describe it. Grief, regret, guilt were all there for him to sample again, except this time his guilt was merited.

'I've tried to call her, to email her—flowers…'

'This is too big for flowers.'

Xante nodded.

'Have you tried writing to her?'

'I told you, I've emailed.'

Despina shook her head. 'I have every one of the letters your father sent me. He lived four streets away, but each Friday when we were courting I ran to the mail box. Letters are different.' She headed off into the house and came back with a pad and envelope, even air-mail stickers and stamps.

'Write,' she said. Wishing him a happy New Year and kissing him goodnight, she went inside.

And Xante discovered letters *were* different. In emails it had been easy to say that he was sorry, just hitting delete when it didn't come out right. It had been so much easier to plead his case and to tell her that they were worth a second chance. But staring at a blank page was different.

It was as well it was a full pad, because it took endless attempts.

The veranda was littered with little white balls of paper, and down to the last page Xante admitted the truth and told her exactly what was on his mind. Then he signed it, addressed the envelope and at three a.m. on New Year's Day walked into the village and posted his letter. He instantly regretted it, hating every word he had written, positive he'd blown what little chance he had.

He hadn't even told her he loved her.

* * *

If she'd done one thing right in her life, this was it.

Confident and gorgeous and brimming with hope, Emily at seventeen was everything Karin hadn't been.

Breezing back at Christmas, she was like a breath of fresh air.

The house minus Matthew was a touch bare, but clean, and there was a maturity to Emily that made Karin proud, that told her the little girl she had spent her life protecting had grown up—and grown up well.

'Of course you have to sell it.'

They were walking around the frozen lake, the trees white from frost; two sisters walking and talking and sorting out their future together.

'There will be talk,' Karin said. 'Once the papers get hold of it and realise just how much in debt we are. Look, I'm just scared of what might come out.'

'Scared they might find out we're not perfect?' Emily smiled, but then her little face was suddenly serious. 'I remember how bad it was, Karin. Not everything, but I do remember the rows. And, even though I didn't know exactly what had happened to you, I knew it was bad.' Karin stood, and

Emily walked a couple of steps ahead before she realised her sister wasn't keeping up. Turning, she walked back and wrapped her arms around her big sister, and for Karin it was as if Emily was suddenly the elder one.

'You know about that?'

'Of course I know.'

'I didn't ever want you to find out.'

'Karin, when I went to boarding school all I felt was relief. I hated that you were still at home. You've looked after me so much; you should be the one taking the money instead of paying for my studies. I know that's why you failed your exams. Keep the rose,' Emily said. 'Or sell it so that you can go back to school—it's time to look after you. I'm all grown up now. And—' she gave a cheeky smile '—relatively unscathed.' She was smiling and crying, not just a sister, but a friend too. 'Thanks to you. You've looked after me, but who's looked after you?'

'I'm fine.'

'What about Xante?' Emily asked.

'That was nothing,' Karin attempted, but her blush gave her away.

'Karin, you'd never go to Greece with a man if he meant nothing.'

'I know,' Karin admitted. 'It just didn't work out in the end.'

"Did you tell him what had happened?'

'No.' Karin shook her head. 'Xante took it upon himself to find out my past.' And she was expecting at least a loyal utterance of 'bastard!' from Emily—only it never came.

'Maybe he thought it was the only way he could find out,' Emily said gently. 'Karin, you've never even spoken about it to me.'

'I was trying to protect you,' Karin snapped.

'Fair enough. But please don't tell me you were trying to protect Xante Rossi by not telling him.'

'No,' Karin said slowly. 'I was trying to protect myself.'

'From what?'

'From this,' Karin said without elaborating, walking across the frozen grass back towards the house. From this endless pain. From loving him only to lose him, and from letting him in, knowing he would one day leave. Oh, he might have accelerated things, but the ending had always been inevitable.

It was a long, cold winter. But because she was a survivor, whether she wanted to be or not, Karin got through it, sorting out her life from the bottom up.

She'd never considered herself a victim, but she didn't want to be a survivor, either; didn't want to label herself in that way. All she wanted now was to get on with the complicated, wonderful task of living. She'd never wanted Xante sweeping up her falling leaves, and there had been too many even for Karin. The house had gone on the market and had sold to a delightful young couple with an army of children.

Change rang in along with the new year.

Karin watched the daffodil shoots peer through the grass around the lake, sampling spring at Omberley Manor for the very last time. And, though it hurt to sign the papers, it didn't hurt as much as she had thought it would. There wasn't much time to be pensive. Karin was way too busy clearing the house of its more dreary contents, choosing what her and Matthew would keep and what could be sold.

She wasn't exactly happy, but there was a marked absence of fear that felt nice. Even Matthew had lifted his game, and although she didn't see him much he did have a job now, and had even sent her a cheque to pay a few of the bills.

There were some good memories, Karin thought as the door knocked and she opened the door to the valuer. And as she walked him through her home and took him through her things, she relived it all. Yes, there were lots of good memories, Karin realised. But there were plenty of bad ones too.

Now she got to choose the ones she kept.

'I'm not selling the rugby memorabilia,' Karin explained to Elliot, the valuer. She attempted businesslike, attempted distance, but she had to pull on every last shred of reserve as she watched him pick up and examine her things, making notes in his pad as he went. She had seen his eyes light up when they had come to the library—all the picture and trophies of her grandfather's glory days were all there on display.

'Pity. There's a huge market for it.' His eyes widened when he saw her grandfather's rose, safely back where it belonged. 'One of these was sold at auction not that long ago; it went for a fortune.'

'Well, this one's not for sale—' Karin said primly, actually managing a small smile to herself, wondering what Elliot would say if he knew it was actually *that* rose that had been sold, and what it had taken to get it back!

'It will be back on the market soon. I'll keep an eye out and let you know what it goes for. It's a great time to sell; the Six Nations is going amazingly. I'll let you know what it goes for, just in case you change your mind.'

'I won't change my mind,' Karin answered, but she was intrigued. It had to be her rose they were talking about; surely there weren't that many out there. 'How do you know it will be back on the market?'

'It's what he always does.' Elliot was holding a leather ball in his hand, besotted with the collection and more than happy to chat if it meant he could linger a little while longer. 'Some rich chap with more money than he knows what to do with. He often buys sports memorabilia, displays them for a while then sells them on.'

'Once he's bored with them.' Karin struggled to keep the edge from her voice. He'd called her so many times since that bitter day, had sent flowers, had even been to the door, but she'd refused to answer. She was still angry with him, but more terrified she might relent and believe in him again, just as so many had. Xante liked to win, liked the chase, the conquest. And, once acquired, when the thrill had gone, he moved on.

Her heart couldn't take it again.

It had been a relief when finally he'd accepted her terse request that he please just leave her alone.

'He likes to change the displays, keep them fresh. He gets a lot of regular guests. It's a bit of a draw card for his hotels. Mind you, he makes sure his things go to a good home...' So they *were* talking about Xante. She was assailed with a sudden vision of all Xante's exes wrapped in shawls, being put out to pasture like unwanted donkeys. 'He gives them to charities. They generally auction them off—nice guy.'

'He gives them to charities?'

'Whoops!' Elliot put down the ball and gave her an apologetic grimace. 'That was very indiscreet of me. Easy to lose your head surrounded by this stuff—it's a collector's dream, you know.'

'Why was that indiscreet?' She handed him a pile of black-and-white photos, and knew she had him.

'He does it all anonymously.' Elliot was entranced by the old photos. 'He just donated a week's training with the England rugby team to some poor inner-city school—and that's not telling tales; it was in the paper. Is that Obolensky?'

'I think so,' Karin said vaguely, her mind just whirring. Everything she had accused him of, everything about him that she had tried to console herself with late at night, she'd got wrong.

'It is!' Elliot squealed. 'Did you know, apparently he liked to have oysters and champagne for breakfast?'

'I didn't know,' Karin laughed.

He was staggeringly indiscreet after that, rifling through the photos. Karin learnt that Xante, far from being a spoilt little rich boy, actually moved most of his things on to charities or museums. 'He even buys back the odd medal, you know, when some of the greats fall on hard times. They sell their stuff, he buys it—and, well, he keeps it for a while then gives it back to the rightful owner. Completely anonymously, that's his rule.'

'Who?' Karin asked. 'Who are the players that he's helped?'

'Now, that really would be indiscreet.' Elliot smiled, and reluctantly he put down the photos. 'If you ever change your mind about selling…'

'I told you, I won't.'

'It's more than money sometimes, isn't it? I know if it were mine I wouldn't be able to part with it.'

And then she did the strangest thing. She took the photo of the great Russian Obolensky and gave it to Elliot. 'That's not for sale,' Karin said. 'That's for you.'

Maybe she'd read Elliot wrong—maybe next week it would appear in an auction—only something told Karin it wouldn't. She understood in that moment that it wasn't all hers to keep, and saw in Elliot's face the very real pleasure that came from giving and sharing those wonderful memories with a nation that held them dear too.

'Thank you.' Elliot clearly didn't know what to say. 'You've no idea what this means…'

He'd no idea what he'd done either—he'd just given her another glimpse of Xante.

'Are you going to the match today?' Karin asked, but Elliot shook his head.

'Couldn't get tickets. I might just wander down to the ground and take a walk around outside; I can feel the pull of the crowd.'

As she waved one very happy buyer goodbye, Karin wondered what Elliot would say if he knew what she'd passed up today. They'd have been heading off soon for their champagne reception and then settling down to watch the rugby match. Heading back to the study, Karin sat for the longest time amongst her grandfather's things, thinking of him and Xante.

Two men who despite different backgrounds were intrinsically the same.

Proud men who excelled. There was a photo of her grandfather on the wall, ball clutched to his chest, fierce concentration in his features, his only goal to win, to conquer. Was that Xante's goal—to have her love him at all costs?

And what then?

There on the mantelpiece, as it had been for weeks now, was the white envelope. She hadn't opened it, but she hadn't shred it into a thousand pieces or tossed it on the fire.

But she'd thought about doing all three.

Karin had deleted his texts unread, had scrolled through his emails and sent them to the junk pile. And though the flowers should have gone in the bin they had been great when the house was being viewed.

There was just something about a letter, though.

His spiky writing was on the envelope, with a Greek postmark, and it had arrived on the fourth of January.

It was March now.

She could see her fingers shaking as she slit open the envelope.

Wondering what, if anything, Xante could say that might change things.

Unfolding the paper, her eyes misted as she smiled.

No apology, no explanations or declarations, because she'd heard them all before.

Just an honest statement from a very proud man, and Karin knew, because she was starting to understand him, just how hard those words would have been to write.

Glancing at the clock, Karin took a deep breath.

If she stepped on it, she might just make it. And maybe, just maybe, so might they.

CHAPTER TWELVE

TODAY, he should be excited about the game. He had two VIP tickets, and to Xante's surprise he had been invited to observe the changing rooms at half time. Yet he couldn't look forward to it.

Today should have been shared with Karin.

He had never gone to anything without a partner. There was any number of women he could have rung, except he hadn't wanted to.

Was this the reason he had never fallen in love before? Xante thought as the English team milled in the foyer. There was a crowd gathered outside his hotel waiting to cheer them on and wish them well, and to the crowd's delight some of the players were outside signing autographs. It was everything Xante wanted for his hotel. London was at its beautiful best, the spring air mild, the skies blue and clear. It should have been the best day, except it barely touched the sides.

Xante had never lost before, had always made it his business to win.

But love chose not to play by his rules.

And it hurt.

The hotel appeared quiet once the team and their entourage departed, except Xante knew better. Behind the scenes the ball room was being prepared, the chefs cooking meals for their return, adding the last touches to the victory cake that might never see the light of day. It was right he should go and see it. His chef was the jewel in the hotel's crown, and the one man Xante occasionally pandered to.

The cake was stunning, an exact replica of the trophy the victors would claim. Somehow Jacques had created its image in spun sugar. Its surface was absolutely smooth like frosted glass, and beneath, a filling made of traditional strawberries and cream. This was perhaps the most elegant strawberry-charlotte cake in history.

But it had come at a cost. The freshness of the ingredients that were now encased in elaborate frosting meant Jacques had been working through the night, his craggy French face quilted in concentration as he added the finishing touches to his masterpiece.

'They must win!' He didn't look up as his boss entered; in fact, he cussed in his own tongue at the intrusion. The chef was one of the few who would swear at Xante and get away with it. 'All this work, and maybe they no see.'

'How does it feel?' Xante asked, curious now as he watched him work. 'When it's cut up?'

'Like serving my guts on a plate and then handing over a carving knife!' the deranged chef raged, but then he gave a rare smile. 'But it is the best feeling too. I remember each beauty I have created with love. This is the best, though. This one will hurt the most!'

Why could everything he said be compared to Karin?

Was this how he must now live, lugging around a broken heart for the rest of his life, accepting defeat as somehow he knew he must?

Except there was no dignity in this defeat, no consolation that he had given his best.

He'd given her his worst. He had set a detective on to her then bullied her into confessing. He didn't blame her for a second for ignoring his attempts at contact, but, oh, how he'd kill for just one more chance.

'What time do you leave?' Jacques asked, and Xante glanced at his watch.

'Ten minutes ago…' He looked again at the cake. 'Congratulations, it's beautiful.'

'*Merci.*'

He thought he was hallucinating as he walked out into the foyer, for there she was—just as she had been on the first day they'd met, walking past Albert, smiling a greeting. It wasn't her assumption that had him intrigued as she walked towards him this time; there was this air of tranquillity about her, an innate strength in her eyes, that took Xante's breath away.

'You came?'

'I accepted the invitation,' Karin said in a matter-of-fact voice. 'It would have been rude not to.'

Was that the only reason she was here?

There was nothing in her eyes that gave him a clue, nothing in her stance that bore witness to all they had shared. Cool, elegant and always beautiful, she stood before him.

But if she was here for them, if somehow he was going to be given another chance, then Xante knew he had to get it right this time.

That it had to be perfect.

'I just have to go to my room.' Xante gave a tight smile. 'And then I'll be ready.'

'No problem.'

Completely unflustered when Xante returned and they headed out, she slid into the car beside him, and they drove in silence the short distance to the ground.

There was no one more skilled at flirting than Xante, yet the skill abandoned him at the very moment he needed it most. He was always together, always assured—always always, always... Suddenly he was as gauche as a teenager and trying not to show it. She was, to him, like glass—he had no idea how to handle her, as if all natural movement had left him, just as if Jacques had told him to move the cake.

A champagne reception in the Orchard enclosure greeted them. Karin surprised Xante by taking a glass, but did not surprise herself. The rigid control she had sworn by had left her the day she'd met Xante, after all. How nice it was to just be herself now, to have found herself, and the absence of fear was surely the best thing in the world to wake up to. She felt safe enough now to be herself and know she wouldn't come to harm.

Sick with nerves on the way to his hotel, she had been dreading seeing him, and dreading not seeing him even more, and it had taken all her control not to rush to him in the foyer. But now they were here, mingling with the crowd, feeling the excitement in the air, it was hard not to relax and enjoy. Eating a sumptuous four-course lunch, listening to the speeches, she caught Xante watching her.

'What?'

'You look happy.'

'I am.' Karin smiled, because finally she was. Finally she had let go of the sordid parts of her past and kept only the good bits, and now she could remember them with love.

'It's nice being back at Twickenham. My grandfather used to bring me here.' They were getting ready to move to their seats for the pre-match entertainment before the three o'clock kick-off that was nearing. 'Before the refurbishment, of course. Sometimes we'd just slip into the stands and watch, other times he'd bring me to the formal functions. I can remember once when we were in the stands, though, and a man nearby suddenly recognised my grandfather. He told him how wonderful he was, and it made his day—just that people remembered him, remembered all he had achieved. Rugby meant everything to him.'

'And his family too,' Xante offered, but Karin shook her head.

'Not in the end.' She gave a small shrug. 'After my grandmother died, they were the one disappointment in an otherwise glorious life, but he *was* proud of me.' It was nice to be able to say it, nice to just speak the truth and accept the love her grandfather had given without the bitter taste of regret.

Xante swallowed. 'I see that you are selling your home.' He had money, so much money. It was a curse sometimes. He knew how pompous he sounded, but whatever the outcome, whatever happened today, he wanted to do one right thing by her. 'You don't have to.'

'Yes, Xante, I do,' she interrupted. 'It's already sold. The exchange takes place next month, and I'm actually relieved. I've spent my whole life trying to honour his memory, trying to claw my way back to what the Wallises once were. I want to do it by myself now. I want to live my life on my terms. I'm hardly going to be in the poor house once the sale goes through...' He saw the flash of tears in her eyes, knew behind the brave words she was bleeding inside—yet he also knew that she meant it. 'It's time to put the past where it belongs.'

It *was* right that she was here today. She had spent so much time protecting her grandfather's heritage that in doing so she had forgotten to protect her own, and now it was time to claim the wonderful future she somehow knew awaited.

Twickenham was the place her grandfather had loved the most. She didn't need a house, or even a rose, to hold onto his memory. She dragged in the air, and could almost feel him standing on the other side of her, sharing in the magnificent sight of his team running out onto the pitch.

The bands were in place, the flags proudly displayed, the teams lined up side by side. England and Scotland, two great nations, were preparing for battle, and the atmosphere was electric.

The Scottish team was standing shoulder to shoulder, bristling with energy, all eager to get out there. But first duty called, and Karin felt her throat tighten and every little hair on the back of her neck stand on end. 'Xante, I have a confession.' She watched as a slight flash of alarm crossed his features—which was merited, given her last confession—and somehow that made her smile.

'You can tell me anything.'

'I love the Scottish anthem, and not just a little bit either.'

She watched and listened as the drums rolled, then beat their slow rhythm. The cry of the bagpipes made her quiver, together with the passion in the crowd as it sang along and as people held up phones, capturing this wonderful anthem for ever.

The rough, passionate faces of the Scottish team were shown on the big screens but blurred before her eyes as the emotional rendition filled the stadium.

Every heartfelt word reached her.

She could feel the man beside her, a man she was so scared to trust but somehow knew she must start to. Her cheeks were wet with tears, her throat tightening as the English national anthem struck up and the crowd raised the roof. The ground filled with one deep, baritone voice as the chests of their beloved team swelled with pride. They stood tall and proud, strapped and ready, brimming with testosterone and singing with a shed-load of passion; it was just a great day to be at Twickenham.

She felt Xante beside her.

She had been born to this.

Xante was here on passion alone, for this great game.

And then came the best bit. Swing Low Sweet Chariot pumped that English blood around her veins, but it was Xante who was singing the loudest.

'Today I am an Englishman trapped in a Greek's body.' He made her smile, he made her laugh; he had made her the woman she'd thought she could never be. 'I love you, Karin.'

He said it just once—looked her right in the eyes as he did so—and then left it to her to do with that knowledge whatever she would.

It was a thrilling match. Just like the old days, she roared her team on, caught up in the rush, watching the ball picked up, tossed, and then caught and held so fiercely. She felt as if they were running with her heart.

And could she do it? Take the risk, throw herself over the line?

Muddied and wearied, still they fought.

Believed the goal was in sight, no matter the score board.

She watched the captain ground the ball, the roar from the crowd fading as they awaited the decision. While the Scots shouted their protest, the English held their breath as the video-referee made his decision—it was just minutes from half time, and this one mattered.

Every single one mattered, but especially this one—because, Karin told herself, if they got this then she'd tell him.

The arm went up, the whistle blew and the try was awarded. The crowd was going wild. The decision had been made for her, only Karin couldn't do it, couldn't just turn around and tell him.

If he gets it over, Karin told herself, *if he converts the try, I'll tell Xante*.

There was a lot more riding on this conversion than the captain realised as he lined up the ball. So badly she wanted that kick to soar between the posts—not just for herself, not just for the team, but for the man who was kicking it.

The man who got up and trained, the man who gave it his all.

There were only winners in this game.

'He'll get it.' Xante had no idea how vital this conversion was, or maybe he did, because he was shouting the ball over as it soared.

And soar it did between the posts, as the crowd roared, a spectacular conversion that had the English singing, and that had Karin tingling right down to her frozen toes. Because now she had to tell him.

'I love you, Xante.' Without qualification, she said it. 'I have always loved you.'

He turned and smiled, because somehow he'd always known that too, had known when he'd held her when they'd been making love. 'You have terrible timing…' He watched her blink at his curious reaction. 'I have been invited to the changing rooms for half time.'

'Oh!'

'You understand, it would be rude…'

'Of course.' Because she did understand. Appearances were everything. Commitments had to be adhered to and, yes, sometimes they were a pain, but now and then they were a pleasure. He took her by the hand and led her through the maze of corridors. Of course they didn't allow Karin in, so she just stood outside listening to the boom of voices and smelling the liniment and the maleness of the place. Her heart thudded in her chest, stunned at how easy it had been to tell him. Stunned at just how good and natural it felt to have told Xante that she loved him.

There were good days and there were best-of-your-life days, and it didn't take being in love to know that this one was extra precious as she flattened against the wall while a wall of muddy men charged past, pumped and ready… And then it was just the two of them.

'Amazing!' He looked like the cat who'd got the cream as he stepped outside, and Karin could only smile.

'Was it great?'

'The best!' Xante nodded. 'You should hear the coach speak; he made you believe that you can do anything.'

'You can.' Karin smiled. 'You do.' Tears pricked her eyes; it was Karin's turn to make an apology.

'What I said that time about you buying friends…' Her skin crawled with shame at the viciousness of her own words. 'I know that's not true. I knew it then, too. They like you because you're knowledgeable, funny, and good and kind…'

'I know.' Xante grinned. 'I'm just glad that you agree.'

'I know who you donated that rugby prize to, too.'

'I can afford to be generous, Karin. When you have so much money, there is the down side that you question people's motives. But on the upside?' He smiled that dangerous smile, the one that always tripped her heart into a gallop. 'Well, there are a lot of upsides!

'Come here.'

He pushed open the door and, like children trespassing, they crept inside. It didn't look particularly hallowed, Karin thought, more like the changing rooms at her old school. But it smelt of men and passion, or was it just that Xante was standing beside her?

He pulled her down onto the bench beside her and put his arm around her. She didn't jump, didn't flinch; instead she just curled into him.

'I love you.' He said it again. 'I think I have loved you from the moment you walked into my hotel. I have never wanted to change or mould you, Karin—all I wanted was the woman you are. I thought I had lost you. Every minute of every day I have wanted to contact you. These last couple of months have been hell, knowing all you were going through and not being able to help you.'

'I had to go through them.' She smiled at his confused face. 'Xante, I had to fix this myself.'

'That row…' She could see the blaze of pain on his face as he recalled it. 'Did I say sorry? Did I tell you how sorry I was for what happened to you? I keep going over and over it, but I can't remember if I did.'

'Yes.' Karin nodded. 'You did. But, way better than that, you didn't let me wallow in my own pity. You were right—it took for ever for me to admit it—but…' She closed her eyes as she summoned her truth. 'You did have a right to know my past when I slept with you. All I can say in my defence is that, yes, I might have been using you. But…' She opened her eyes and he was still there. 'I loved you by then, too. I *had* to have loved you then, Xante, because otherwise it could never have happened like it did.'

He pulled out a little black box and she felt her world still. She could hear the crowd singing outside as he opened it, and she saw the most perfect ring, tiny rubies delicately crafted into a rose.

Her ring.

'You might prefer a diamond.' For the first time ever there was uncertainty in his voice. 'We can change it.' And it seemed right,

Karin reflected, that he wasn't worried she might say no, that he knew as she did that this love was for ever.

'You've been carrying this around all this time?'

'No.' Xante shook his head and placed it on her finger, right where it belonged. 'That is why I had to go back to my room.'

'Not to kick out the blonde?'

'There's been no one else since you, Karin.'

She believed him.

Absolutely she believed him. This delectable man, this playboy made good, would be hers, scars and neurosis and all.

It was Karin's turn for the truth.

'Xante, I can't show you my scars.'

'You don't have to.'

'I just get scared sometimes.'

'So, tell me when you do.'

'It's not that simple.'

'It can be.'

He was kissing her, soft, tender kisses that she'd longed for. But a wooden bench didn't allow for much contact so, still kissing, they stood instead and she was back in his arms where she belonged. And then it changed. The switch tripped, like every time he touched her, just waving away all her doubts and fears.

Oh, and the air was thick with testosterone all right. Xante's hand crept up her skirt, his body pressing into hers. On paper it might not have been the most romantic place in the world, being pushed into a cubicle by a six-foot-two Greek lover, but to Karin it was…

'You'll miss the match.' She was kicking off her panties as she grappled with his belt.

'The boys would understand.'

She'd forgotten just how good he was. Good enough for them both, at least till she caught up. He pressed her to the changing-room wall; she'd forgotten too just how fabulous *it* was, how strong he was as he lifted her. Her legs wrapped around his waist, his breath hot on her neck, and the passion chased every last doubt away…

Leaning on his shoulder as the world trickled back in, she could hear the roar of the crowd outside. A crescendo was building, a humungous roar, that didn't quite match the still peace she felt inside.

'Come on.' Karin smiled. 'Something big is happening out there.'

'Something big just happened in here.' There was no embarrassment as quickly they dressed, Xante doing the honours and darting his head outside. 'They'll be coming in soon to prepare the room…'

'It's not a hotel!' Karin laughed as they ran outside.

'It's—the—changing room—at—Twickenham.' Xante spelt out each word. 'Way better than a hotel—it is hallowed ground.' They were running through the tunnels, climbing the steps to the stands, and then they stopped for a moment to share a wild grin.

'Wasn't it great.' She wasn't asking a question.

'The best,' Xante admitted, the perfect proposal executed beyond even his wildest dreams. Seeing her stand there, blonde hair tumbling, her cheeks flushed, he knew only sweet secrets would be their bedfellows now. 'The very best!' he affirmed, and, taking her hand, he led her back into the crowd, blending into this mass of passionate singing that carried her home.

EPILOGUE

OH, SHE still had her moments.

Her wishes might have been granted—but love, despite the propaganda that surrounded it, actually wasn't a magic wand.

Love didn't take away every last neurosis.

Love didn't creep in at four a.m. and tap you on the shoulder to remind you that you were safe. No, love wrapped you in its arms at two minutes past four and patiently waited for the nightmare to abate.

Love took hard work from both sides to really make it work.

And love, Karin was fast learning, could always make you laugh.

Even at things you never thought you would have.

'Who's complaining?' Xante sat up in the rumpled bed, blinking as her panic attack had awoken him, and only teasing her when he knew that she was ready to be teased. 'I have a woman who prefers the lights on when we make love, one who knows more about rugby than me,' Xante continued with a nudge.

'I do,' Karin said with a self-satisfied smile. 'I'm going to get a drink; do you want one?'

Xante yawned and shook his head as Karin slipped out of bed and padded to the kitchen. She was five months' pregnant. They knew they were having a boy, and Karin was sure he was going to follow in his grandfather's footsteps, because his little feet regularly kicked her awake.

She rubbed some cream into her scar; it was itching like crazy as her stomach slowly stretched. She was dreading labour. Pregnancy was made so much harder with the midwives and doctors looking at her body— though her obstetrician had told her that once she had had the baby he would refer her to a cosmetic surgeon, because there was a lot that could be done. The thought of Xante seeing her scars for the first time during labour made her feel sick. Still, instead of dwelling on it she poured some milk, drinking it down and then topping up her

glass before pouring one for Xante—
because, if she didn't, he would no doubt
ask for a swig of hers and then drink the lot!

She'd had no intention of going to the
study, but the open door seemed to call her.
Walking in, the room was familiar enough
that the darkness didn't faze her as she put
down the glasses and flicked on the table
lamp.

It was her favourite room in the gorgeous
home they'd bought in Twickenham. It was
bigger than the cottage she'd initially chosen,
and rather more expensive. But it wasn't
showy, and it wasn't stately, and Karin knew,
stroking her kicking bump, that it would
never, ever be a burden.

Her grandfather's treasures suited the
room, mingling now with treasured memories of her own: their wedding day.

Despina's first of many visits to London.

She had a friend now, a widower from the
island she had shyly introduced. A lawyer
who would have been a rival in business
now, had Xante followed his parents'
dreams.

Instead he was becoming a firm and respected friend.

Colour hadn't dashed in for Despina.

Instead, neutral colours had replaced her black uniform—cream stockings, beige lip-glosses and now the occasional pale blouse—but colour *was* returning. Rainbows always followed rain, Karin realised now, if only you looked out for them.

Yes, new memories were being created every day.

Karin Rossi was finding her feet, and discovering that, if you opened up and let it in, the world was actually quite forgiving and kind. Life was a vast circle that you either closed off and ignored, or gingerly stepped into and let it sweep you away.

She went to flick off the light, but the rose caught her eye—and then the letter that lay beneath it.

She read it, not often, just sometimes when she was happy, and always when she was sad, or when Xante was away on business and the house seemed too big for her alone.

And on this cold, grey morning, as the heating cranked on, Karin read it again.

Read the single line that had won her heart.

His honesty was as palpable now as it had been the first day she'd read it.

That Xante Rossi—who always had the answer, always had a back-up plan—could so concisely describe his world without *them*.

I don't know what to do.
Xante

No kiss had followed his name, no presumption, no promises, just an honest admission, and one Karin could relate to.

Reading his words for the thousandth time, that last little piece of her heart was given over to him.

She trusted him.

Always she had loved him, but now, six months' married and pregnant with his son, truly she trusted him.

Love was a gift that was just a given—but trust was a treasured reward.

Trust—easy for the naïve, but, oh, so much harder for the jaded.

Her baby was still; his kicks had been fading for a little while now. Karin cuddled him asleep, holding her tummy till the little rhythms faded, and then she did the bravest thing ever. She pulled off her cami and, flicking off the light, she picked up their milk and walked to the bedroom safe in her new knowledge and only a teeny bit scared.

She trusted him, and it felt fantastic.

Xante, unaware of the seismic shift that had occurred, had the nerve to be asleep and didn't even wake as she placed his glass on the table and crawled in bed beside him. He just lay, snoring softly, grabbing those last, precious minutes before the day demanded him.

'Xante!' She dug him in the ribs and he mumbled an apology, rolling on his side and promptly falling back to sleep, his loose arm crashing over her body, and his hand, as it always did, heading for the usual resting-place of her left breast.

Only this time it was bare.

She felt his hand stiffen for a second, and so too did Karin. She wondered what he would do, what he would say—or, worst, wondered if he would pretend not to notice, or say it didn't matter.

Because it did matter.

She held his hand and guided him to feel it, and turned away from him, because it was easier than watching as for the first time she let him explore.

'Can I see?'

So she let him. She let him turn on the sidelight, and watched the tears in his eyes as he took it all in—and then he kissed it. Kissed all the hurt and pain, and if love could have erased it then Karin would have looked down to find it gone.

'I'm sorry for all that happened to you. I am so sorry that it did. But it made you who you are, Karin; it made you strong.'

'I know.'

'And you are beautiful.'

'Not like this.'

'Yes,' Xante said. 'Your grandfather had scars; did it make you love him less?'

'No.'

'They told a tale—and these tell yours.'

His fingers were cool and stopped the burning itching, and it felt so strange but so nice to be utterly naked, not to have the itch of fabric on her scars.

'It won't.' Karin cleared her throat. 'It won't put you off…?'

'Hey, you're talking to a Greek boy.' Xante grinned, holding her wrists over her head and pinning her down with his mouth. 'Not some namby-pamby boy playing soldiers…'

She was laughing and crying and doing

that stupid wrestling thing, rather stunned to realise that they were over that hurdle, that the mountain she had envisaged wasn't even a molehill; it was nothing at all. Just another part of her that Xante had long ago accepted. And clearly it wasn't going to affect his ardour; clearly, because something was rapidly nudging awake against her leg, just as it did every single morning.

'Does nothing stop you?'

'Nothing.' Xante grinned. 'So you'd better just get used to it.'

She attempted a martyred sigh, only she was smiling too much to manage it.

'I love you, Karin.'

He wasn't playing and he wasn't joking. He loved her—it was as simple and as complicated as that.

Love was a lesson she'd happily spend for ever learning.

* * * * *

Turn the page for an exclusive extract from
THE PRINCE'S CAPTIVE WIFE
by
Marion Lennox

Bedded and wedded—by blackmail!

Nine years ago Prince Andreas Karedes left Australia to inherit his royal duties, but unbeknownst to him he left a woman pregnant.

Innocent young Holly tragically lost their baby and remained on her parents' farm to be near her tiny son's final resting place, wishing Andreas would return!

A royal scandal is about to break: a dirt-digging journalist has discovered Holly's secret, so Andreas forces his childhood sweetheart to come and face him! Passion runs high as Andreas issues an ultimatum: to avoid scandal, Holly must become his royal bride!

"She was only seventeen?"

"We're talking ten years ago. I was barely out of my teens myself."

"Does that make a difference?" The uncrowned king of Aristo stared across his massive desk at his younger brother, his aquiline face dark with fury. "Have we not had enough scandal?"

"Not of my making." Prince Andreas Christos Karedes, third in line to the Crown of Aristo, stood his ground against his older brother with the disdain he always used in this family of testosterone-driven males. His father and brothers might be acknowledged womanizers, but Andreas made sure his affairs were discreet.

"Until now," Sebastian said. "Not counting your singularly spectacular divorce, which had a massive impact. But this is worse. You will have to sort it before it explodes over all of us."

"How the hell can I sort it?"

"Get rid of her."

"You're not saying…"

"Kill her?" Sebastian smiled up at his younger brother, obviously rejecting the idea—though a tinge of regret in his voice said the option wasn't altogether unattractive.

And Andreas even sympathized. Since their father's death, all three brothers had been dragged through the mire of the media spotlight, and the political unrest was threatening to destroy them. In their thirties, impossibly handsome, wealthy beyond belief, indulged and feted, the brothers were now facing realities they had no idea what to do with.

"Though if I was our father…" Sebastian added, and Andreas shuddered. Who knew what the old king would have done if he'd discovered Holly's secret? Thank God he'd never found out. Not that King Aegeus could have taken the moral high ground. It was, after all, his father's past actions that had gotten them into this mess.

"You'll make a better king than our father ever was," Andreas said softly. "What filthy dealing made him dispose of the royal diamond?"

"That's my concern," Sebastian said. There could be no royal coronation until the diamond was found—they all knew that—but the way the media was baying for blood there might not be a coronation even then. Without the diamond the rules had changed. If any more scandals broke... "This girl..."

"Holly."

"You remember her?"

"Of course I remember her."

"Then she'll be easy to find. We'll buy her off—do whatever it takes, but she mustn't talk to anyone."

"If she wanted to make a scandal she could have done it years ago."

"So it's been simmering in the wings for years. To have it surface now..." Sebastian rose and fixed Andreas with a look that was almost as deadly as the one used by the old king. "It can't happen, brother. We have to make sure she's not in a position to bring us down."

"I'll contact her."

"You'll go nowhere near her until we're sure of her reaction. Not even a phone call, brother. For all we know her phones are already tapped. I'll have her brought here."

"I can arrange…"

"You stay right out of it until she's on our soil. You're heading the corruption inquiry. With Alex on his honeymoon with Maria— of all the times for him to demand to marry, this must surely be the worst—I need you more than ever. If you leave now and this leaks, we can almost guarantee losing the crown."

"So how do you propose to persuade her to come?"

"Oh, I'll persuade her," Sebastian said grimly. "She's only a slip of a girl. She might be your past, but there's no way she's messing with our future."

* * * * *

Be sure to look for
THE PRINCE'S CAPTIVE WIFE
by Marion Lennox,
available September 2009
from Harlequin Presents®!

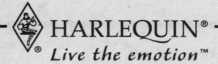

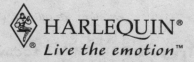

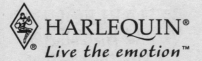

HARLEQUIN®
INTRIGUE®

BREATHTAKING ROMANTIC SUSPENSE

Shared dangers and passions lead to electrifying
romance and heart-stopping suspense!

Every month, you'll meet six new heroes
who are guaranteed to make your spine tingle
and your pulse pound. With them you'll enter
into the exciting world of Harlequin Intrigue—
where your life is on the line
and so is your heart!

THAT'S INTRIGUE—
ROMANTIC SUSPENSE
AT ITS BEST!

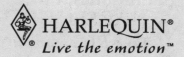

HARLEQUIN®
Live the emotion™

HARLEQUIN®

Super Romance®

...there's more to the story!

Superromance.
A *big* satisfying read about unforgettable
characters. Each month we offer *six* very different
stories that range from family drama to adventure
and mystery, from highly emotional stories to
romantic comedies—and much more! Stories
about people you'll believe in and care about.
Stories too compelling to put down....

Our authors are among today's *best* romance
writers. You'll find familiar names and talented
newcomers. Many of them are award winners—
and you'll see why!

If you want the biggest and best
in romance fiction, you'll get it
from Superromance!

Exciting, Emotional, Unexpected...

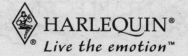

HARLEQUIN®
Live the emotion™

Harlequin® Historical
Historical Romantic Adventure!

*Imagine a time of chivalrous
knights and unconventional ladies,
roguish rakes and impetuous
heiresses, rugged cowboys
and spirited frontierswomen—
these rich and vivid tales will
capture your imagination!*

*Harlequin Historical . . .
they're too good to miss!*

HHDIR06

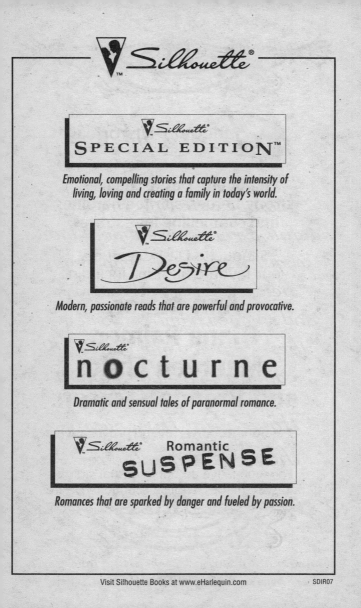

❖ Silhouette®

❖ Silhouette®
SPECIAL EDITION™

Emotional, compelling stories that capture the intensity of living, loving and creating a family in today's world.

❖ Silhouette®
Desire

Modern, passionate reads that are powerful and provocative.

❖ Silhouette®
nocturne

Dramatic and sensual tales of paranormal romance.

❖ Silhouette® Romantic
SUSPENSE

Romances that are sparked by danger and fueled by passion.

passionate powerful provocative love stories

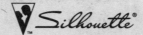

**Silhouette Desire® delivers
strong heroes, spirited heroines
and compelling love stories.**

Silhouette Desire features
your favorite authors, including

Ann Major,
Diana Palmer,
Maureen Child
and Brenda Jackson.

**Passionate, powerful and provocative
romances *guaranteed!***

For superlative authors, sensual stories
and sexy heroes, choose Silhouette Desire.

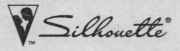

passionate powerful provocative love stories